# **<u>Chapter 1</u>**

I needed this so badly. After weeks of being locked in my room, worrying about Jason and what he was doing now that he was single. I wanted to get out, see the snow, and enjoy the cabin with my friends this weekend. It would be a hell of a lot easier if he wasn't a mutual friend and *joining* us. Truth is, he wasn't a bad guy, by any means. Jason had a lot of redeemable qualities: his love for animals, and apparently his newfound love of screwing my best friend Macy.

I know, right? I can't blame her, as Macy tends to lose all sense of her inhibitions when the Jack Daniels gets poured. No. I blame him. But this weekend wasn't about him. It couldn't be. I had to focus on myself, my friends, and at least attempt to have a decent time.

"ARE YOU READY TO HIT THE SLOOOOOPES?!"

*Brandon. You could always see him before you heard him. One of his trademarks.*

"Brandon! My mom is home, and you know how she feels about your less than quiet inside voice," I scolded.

"Sorry, are you packed?"

"You bet. I just want to drink, ski, and pretend I'm not a black hole of sadness for a few days," I sighed.

And with that pathetic truth being spoke into existence, we loaded the van already filled with Erica, Joey, Macy, and... Jason. Oh joy. I opted to sit in the passenger seat as a way to avoid having to look at or be anywhere near him for the next three-hour ride to the cabin.

We have all been friends for years, which is truly spectacular if you realize just how different we all are. Erica is queen bee at our school, all the girls want to be her, and all the guys want to be *with* her. With her long blonde hair and bright blue eyes, who wouldn't? She encompasses a beautiful and given soul, but she can kind of be a little reserved. I have always said that she seems as if she is holding in an enormous secret at all times. She is on the tall side, which most of the guys at our school would find intimidating- but don't due to the fact that she is probably the most popular.

*What's not to love?*

Joey is a handsome olive-skinned basketball all-star with the sweetest heart, and a killer smile. He's also been my best guy friend for as long as I can remember. Joey is one of the most well-liked people I know. In fact, I don't think there is a single soul at our school, let alone on Earth that holds any grievances towards him. He is incredibly personable and doesn't let his popularity get to his head.

Macy's a drop-dead gorgeous brunette with a kind heart, captain of the debate team, and also my best friend since we were in diapers. She has the kindest brown eyes, which sparkle whenever she begins to talk about something that excites her. I trust her with my life, and I know she would do anything for me- without hesitation.

Brandon has sandy blonde hair, brown eyes, and one of the loudest voices I have ever heard. He can sure light up a room, in fact, that was his specialty. He is probably the tallest out of all of us, which is staggering when you realize Jason is over six feet alone. He wasn't the athletic type, but this guy was a tank. It almost seemed ironic, given the fact the he had a generous, and kind heart.

Where do I begin with Jason? Jason is pretty much a six-foot two Greek god, and I'm not exaggerating. His emerald green eyes can catch your attention from across the room, and they go perfectly with his year-round perfect tan. He also has a love for books, reading, and writing which pairs exactly with my interests. We love to curl up in a cozy armchair and get lost in a great book. Okay, he's perfect, besides the fact that he's a cheater.

*Geez, Avery. Resentful much?*

I'm Avery. I have ash blonde hair, green eyes, less than perfect skin, and a love for books. We are a crazy bunch but somehow, we all work. We all support, forgive, and love one other despite our obvious differences.

It was a loud car ride, surprisingly not due to Brandon, but mostly attributed to Erica practically shouting about how she was going to look, "like an absolute snow bunny and needed great posts for Instagram, and all her followers would be just SO jealous." I think she also mentioned the word hashtag, but isn't that every other word out of these Instagram influencers mouths? I was grateful however, because funnily enough her voice was loud enough to distract me momentarily from how absolutely *wonderful* Jason smelled. It was a scent I was familiarized with and had never realized just how much I was attracted to it, until we weren't together anymore.

*That was the worst day of my life to date.*

When I found out about what had happened, I felt absolutely crushed. My boyfriend of two years, and the person I told everything to did without a doubt the worst thing he could ever do to me. He claimed he was drunk, but so was Macy. So, who did I blame? Knowing how Macy gets, I gave her the benefit of the doubt and a pass despite the depravity of the situation. She's been my best friend since we were in diapers and had never done anything even remotely terrible to me up until that point. She was also the one who told me about what had happened, so there's points there.

The weird bit is about the whole situation is that those two haven't been on great terms either. I always thought of them as close friends, and two people who just clicked exceptionally well. However, since the incident there's been a rift between them. The interesting part? The coldness is one-sided and is coming all from Jason.

I have seen Macy try and discuss what happened as a way to move past it. However, he seems to want nothing to do with reconciliation or even her in general. A small part of me is happy. If they had become a couple after him and I separated, it would have definitely added salt to the already deep wound. On the other hand, while I forgave her, I know it was both of their fault and don't understand his reasoning behind the coldness. Sometimes when I let my mind wander, I wonder if somet...

"WE'RE HERE!!!"

My darkest thoughts were interrupted by Brandon's high-pitched scream letting us all know that we had in fact, arrived. The cabin was breathtaking. All a dark espresso wood in a classic cabin style. There was even a beautiful white brick chimney dusted with the most delicate white snow. This was exactly what I needed.

We all began to file out one by one grabbing our luggage from the back. Brandon grabbed the key, and let us all in. I remembered I left my charger in the car and jogged out to Brandon's blue sedan. As I was closing the door, I turned around and almost ran right into Jason.

"Excuse me, I left my backpack," he said.

"No worries."

"Avery..." he pleaded.

"No. I can be friendly with everyone together, but I can't do this part with you. Not anymore Jason. You saw to that," I responded harshly.

His face turned somber, and he stepped aside and let me pass. No. I would not feel sorry for him. He did this to himself! I would have done anything for him. If I was being honest however, he did look remorseful. That does nothing to change the fact that I am still harboring a broken heart, one that he caused. I wouldn't let anything happen between us. Never again.

As I stepped into the brightly lit home, I gasped. It was decorated with the most beautiful Christmas decorations, granted it wasn't for another couple weeks. There were wreaths decorated with velvet red bows, and a massive eight foot tree in the corner covered with gold, shimmery green, and bright yellow bulbs. The tree was accented with a large shining star perfectly placed at the top of the tree. This was my absolute favorite time of year.

I headed up the stairs to one of two bedrooms. One room had three full beds, which would obviously be for the girls. Out of curiosity, I peeked in the boy's bedroom which was complete with a bunk bed and queen. Just as I was leaving, I saw Jason in the bathroom. He was shirtless and putting away all of his things. I forgot how chiseled his chest was... oh who am I kidding? That is a body you don't forget easily. My inner thoughts then easily became overshadowed with the thought of him and Macy- and that she too saw him the way I have.

I sprinted down the stairs and almost knocked Erica onto the ground in the process.

"Excuse you, Avery! I almost dropped my Chanel purse- and you KNOW how much it means to me!"

"I'm sorry, Erica. Hey, I left you the bed at the farthest to the wall- just the way you like," I said with an apologetic smile.

And just like that she continued walking up the stairs. In the kitchen, Brandon, Macy and Joey were unpacking all the food we bought beforehand from Joey's dad's grocery store. Things that needed to be refrigerated like meats would need to be bought later. In fact, that would be the next thing on our agenda considering it was already mid-day and we would more than likely be staying at the house for the remainder.

"Hey Joey, did you want to drive me to the store? I need to get some meat for us to cook for dinner," I smiled.

"Sure thing, Aves. Leave in 15?"

I nodded and smiled letting him know that was good. Macy didn't acknowledge me the whole time I was down there, and it was bugging me. I know it had been pretty awkward recently, and it was all due to her and my boyfrie... EX boyfriend and their indiscretions. Nevertheless, I had decided to look past it at least for her sake. So why was she being so standoffish? Maybe the thought of the three of us being in the same house for the weekend racked her nerves. In that case, we were on the same boat.

Pushing my negative thoughts aside and determined to have a good day, I jogged up the stairs to change out of my clothes. What is it about road trips that make me feel so dirty? I found a fresh pair of sweats and slipped them on along with my varsity sweater that miraculously still fit and some snow boots. I was about to close the door when I noticed something black and leathery like sticking out from my pillow.

Naturally curious, I walked forward to see what it was. Perhaps something left by the previous occupants or the owners. I lifted up the pillow and let out a high-pitched scream that surely the neighbors would hear. There had to be about 10 cockroaches scrambling in all directions falling off the bed and traveling further into the sheets.

All at once, everyone came running into the room.

"What happened?"

"Aves, are you okay?!"

I stepped back and grabbed Macy and squeezed hard. She was the one person who knew just how afraid I was of bugs and gave me a comforting squeeze in return. I explained the situation to everyone and watched as Jason started stomping all of those nasty filthy insects and gave me a sympathetic smile.

"You ready to go Joey," I said as I forced myself to tear my eyes away from Jason's painfully beautiful face.

With a nod, he let me know he was, and we headed out the door, into the car, and on our way. The drive was silent, but it was comfortable. I never felt awkward around Joey. We had been around each other all our lives as our parents were practically family. I caught him continue to steal glances at me until he sighed and said, "You know I love you. That's why I hate to see you hurting. Are you as okay as you try to make everyone else think you are?"

"No. But I know that what Jason and I had is over. So, I am going through the motions of losing him romantically, while also facing the fact that he will always be in my life... as friends," I said with a sad smile.

I don't know how, but he bought it. With that believable scripted sentence, and his security of knowing I was okay at least for now, Joey continued our comfortable silence until we reached the store. We browsed up and down the aisles for the meats, and condiments we would need to make a makeshift "BBQ" on the stove in the kitchen.

When we got back home, everyone was assembled haphazardly around the small coffee table engaged in a heated UNO match. Naturally, Brandon seemed to be the clear-cut winner as always. Erica, the sore loser, was accusing him of cheating while the tension between Macy and Jason could be cut with a knife. Ah, a typical Friday night.

With Joey and I being the only two able to cook a decent meal, we immediately got to work. The drive to the cabin was tense and everyone was starving. I don't know if it was the tension with Jason, or an attempt to bond with me, but Macy volunteered to help me cook. When dinner was ready, I let everyone make their plates as I loaded the dishwasher.

Macy was being my little helper again and handing me the cooking tools. I reached over my shoulder as she handed me the pan that we cooked the sausages in. She placed the part that had heat on it directly in my palm, and I instantly dropped the pan and examined my now burning palm. She immediately started doling out apologies and helping me run my fingers under the cool water.

I know it was a mistake, but part of me was pissed off. Not only because Macy burnt me, but because Jason was now looking at me in a way that would easily make me putty in his hands. I told everyone to enjoy their meal and took a plain hotdog upstairs, locked the room, and sat on Erica's bed because there's no way in hell I was sitting on that cockroach infested bed of mine again.

My ever-rampant curiosity got the best of me, and I started looking under Erica and Macy's sheets to check for more cockroaches. Funnily enough, there was none. Why was my bed the only one infested? I started turning myself into an amateur detective. Would someone be messing with me? If so, who? I looked under my bed and found what must have been a month-old pizza crust, with surprise, more cockroaches. That explains the filthy insects. I felt so ridiculous. I could barely look Jason in the eye, couldn't have a normal conversation with my best friend, and now had a fleeting thought that one of my closest friends was sabotaging me. I really needed a drink. I was tired of sulking.

I headed down the stairs and was immediately greeted by a groveling Macy, ready with a hundred more apologies. I laughed. She really was such a sweet soul, so I hugged her and told her for the *tenth* time that it was okay. She grinned, gave me a big hug and pulled me into their new game they were playing- truth or dare. How could that go wrong?

They had already started playing, so I took that opportunity to indulge myself in one of my favorite cocktails- a vodka cranberry. I headed into the kitchen. A drink was just what I needed to erase the weird day I had, as well as allowing me to just let loose and have fun with my friends.
"Bad day?"

I turned around. "Jason. Shouldn't you be accepting a dare from Brandon forcing you to lick the carpet or something equally horrible?"
"I suppose I should. I much rather hang out with you though. In fact, it's the reason I came on this trip."

I couldn't hide my shock, but quickly forced the emotion off my face.

"You don't like hanging out with me. In fact, you hated it so much you decided to bang my best friend at a party while I was home studying."

He flinched as if I slapped him.

"Avery, please. I know what I did was wrong. I know it was even worse that it was with Macy, trust me I know. But you know me, her and I are good friends. Why would I do that to you? I think something else was going on that night…"

*I was so sick of his worthless excuses.*

"Like what? You know what- save it. I don't need to hear any more excuses. You better hope you don't pick truth," and with that I stormed into the living room.

"MY TURN," I practically shouted at my friends.

They all erupted into laughter, especially after glancing at the cup I seemed to be clenching in my hand. They all loved drunk Avery, and lucky for them I was a lightweight. I couldn't deal with Jason right now. I decided on a safe person to pick.

*This would be fun.*

"Joey, truth or dare?"

# **<u>Chapter 2</u>**

"Aw Aves. You know me. I'm a dare man all the way," Joey smirked.

"Let's prove it, shall we? Kiss Erica." I laughed. I knew he secretly had a thing for her and wanted to help him out. What are friends for?

Everyone was quiet as Erica flipped her long blonde hair over her shoulder, crawled over to Joey, and grabbed his face. He immediately slammed his lips on hers and it seemed the sexual tension brewing between them for years was finally exposing itself.

They finally pulled away after about 10 seconds and looked immediately embarrassed. Joey's golden cheeks turned bright pink as well as Erica's. Brandon was the first to speak up.

"Alright Avery, now it's Joey's turn to ask you."

Joey looked up, laughed, and said, "Although that will be hard to follow, the man is right. Truth or dare, Avery?"

For the first time since the game started, I began to fret over which one I would pick. Truth is a safe pick, because I would remain sure that no one could force me to do something hauntingly embarrassing. That's why everyone, including myself, was shocked when I blurted out,

"Dare."

It was obvious that Joey was taken aback, and fully prepared with a question assuming I would've taken my normal "safe" route and gone with truth. Nevertheless, he quickly recollected himself and said,

"Okay…it's your turn to kiss someone. Jason?"

"No," I said without an ounce of hesitation.

"Avery, if you don't complete your dare- you're out."

Tired of giving Jason the satisfaction, and not wanting him to be the reason I lose this stupid game of Truth or Dare; I walk over to him. There would be no ten seconds or passion like there was with Erica and Joey. This was dead. I grabbed him and leaned in. The second our lips touched; the spark resurfaced. Although, compared to the spark I felt in our relationship- this felt more like a wildfire… burning throughout my whole-body bringing warmth to all my limbs and making me feel alive. This is wrong. I pulled my body back.

"Alright, who's next?"

Everyone was sitting with their jaws open, with laughter hiding behind a smile, besides Macy. She almost looked… upset. I should have known going into this weekend that it was going to an issue between the three of us at some point. She got up and immediately bolted up the stairs. I know they weren't together, but it must have felt awkward for her. She was still my best friend, and I would hate for any conflict between us. So, I followed her.

The door was locked, but I knocked softly and told her it was me. She was reluctant but came and opened up the door for me.

"Hey Mace, can I talk to you?"

"Of course, I'm sorry for making a scene. It was just awkward considering the issues between all of us. The fact that he was my friend and is now icing me out over a mutual mistake is also wearing on me a little more than I would like to admit."

"I'm sorry. I didn't think about your feelings and how new this is for all of us. But it is just a stupid game. The issues between us three are long over. While I don't see us ever being a couple again, I do forgive him in a way. You have always been forgiven, Mace. Please don't feel weird."

We continued our long-needed conversation for the next hour, until Macy fell asleep in her bed. I was started to feel thirsty from all the alcohol I'd consumed that I went downstairs for some water. Everyone was either passed out in the other bedroom or somewhere on the living room floor. As I was getting water, I saw Jason getting up from the couch. He started to head upstairs before seeing me and changing his course.

"You're still up? Look Avery, I'm sorry about that dare. I don't know why Joey would go there considering. But… you can't tell me you didn't feel that."

"Feel what Jason? There is nothing between us, and never will be again."

"Why is it you tell everyone that both Macy and I are forgiven, but treat me as if I'm not? I understand you can't trust me anymore. We are friends though, aren't we? If not, I would rather go home now then feel as if you hate me for the rest of this trip. I feel like I am walking on eggshells around you. I can't take it."

In that moment, I realized how much of an absolute jerk I had been. Yeah, he made a mistake. So did Macy. However, I decided long ago that I wouldn't let it ruin our friend group, because it was simply much too important to me. If Jason was going to make an effort to be friends, so was I.

"I know you don't want to talk about it Avery, but I don't even remember that night. I woke up next to Macy. But, the last thing I remember was taking a sip of the drink and boom- nothing."

I found myself laughing. "Of course, it's alcohol. That drink was probably your first of many."

"That's the thing though. Joey was also at that party, and said he only saw me drink one."

"Look, if this friendship is going to work, we are going to have to leave the past and the past. This weekend can be our fresh slate. Deal?"

"Deal."

He reached out and took me in his arms. I can't lie, the way it felt, the way he felt, I just knew that I wanted to be more than friends. Regardless, friends are what we were striving for, and I couldn't lose sight of the picture.

Suddenly, I wasn't tired.

"Jason, want to go in the hot tub?"

"In freezing weather? Of course. Let me get my suit."

Fifteen minutes later, we were enjoying the calming effects that only hot water can bring. The bubbles, the tranquil air, the cold breeze- it was perfect. It was a great way for me to unwind after the seemingly stressful day I had.

"You excited to ski tomorrow, Aves?"

"Are you kidding me? You know at this point, I'm basically a champ."

"A champ has to beat the best, and safe to say I'm the best."

"I guess we will have to see about that then... wow is it one a.m. already? We should probably go to bed. I have to preserve my strength to fully kick your ass tomorrow."

We pulled our relaxed bodies out of the water in a fit of laughter over who was the better skier. He got out first and extended his hand to help me out. The feeling of his hand holding mine was electric. Which is why I leaned forward and grabbed his face.

"Avery, what are you doing? I thought we said friends."

"We are. Consider it our final goodbye to the relationship..."

Before I could continue my "we're better as friends" monologue I had set in my head, his mouth came crashing down on mine. I grabbed his hair as he scooped me in his arms and wrapped my legs around his waist. He carried me inside and laid me down on the couch. We continued kissing, but I eventually stopped it because my judgement decided to start working. I realized we weren't alone, but it seems that everyone woke up and made their way back into the bedrooms. I breathed a sigh of relief.

"Thanks for the amazing "goodbye"."

"Anytime beautiful... I mean "friend". Now go get some sleep and rest up. Losing is hard on the body," he winked. He continued, "By the way Aves, you can sleep in my bed tonight. I know the cockroaches really freaked you out. I'll take the couch."

Before I could protest that it wasn't what just friends would have done, he quickly changed and laid down on the couch.

I went up the stairs and into the bathroom to change into some warm clothes. I heard someone stirring in the room and peeked my head out, but both Macy and Erica were sound asleep. I brushed my teeth and my hair and headed into the boys room, and laid down in Jason's bed. And slowly, my eyelids grew heavier and I was out.

I woke to Macy shaking me.

"What are you doing in Jason's bed? Did something happen?"

"No... but he thought I wouldn't want to sleep with cockroaches. He's on the couch," I said still half-asleep.

She simply strutted off in her navy-blue ski outfit. Weird. I decided to finally pull myself up and get ready for the day. I could already hear everyone downstairs, *especially Brandon.*

I went next door to my room, and started to open my suitcase, when my hand was sopping wet. I pulled it all the way open and saw that all of my clothes were completely drenched. I looked up to see if maybe the roof leaked, but nothing was there and the carpet everywhere else was completely dry.

I decided my clothes were a bust, and went downstairs to look for a dryer- much to no avail. I did find everyone at the counter already in their clothes.

"Aves, why aren't you dressed? We have to leave in 10 minutes!" Joey shouted.

"When I woke up, all of my clothes and my suitcase was drenched!"

Everyone was really confused, until I showed them. They all agreed it was weird but decided that maybe it got wet on the way in and I didn't realize until it was too late. I was still too tired to disagree, so I went along with that ridiculous excuse.

Macy, being the sweetheart she is, told me she brought an extra ski outfit that I was welcome to use. Thank god for us being the same size and height. I quickly changed, had my necessary morning cup of coffee and we were all ready to go.

After last night's heart-to-heart with Jason, the seating arrangement in the car was much different. He opted to sit next to me, and my heart was racing a hundred miles a minute. How pathetic was I? Thankfully, nobody suspected anything out of the ordinary between him and I, but I did put on a good front with him as it was. It was only about a twenty-minute ride to the base of the mountain, and then we were there.

We paid for our lift tickets, and then separated into partners. Just call me a matchmaker, because to no one's surprise- Joey and Erika chose to sit with each other. Macy called dibs on Jason, but he told her that he wanted to have a race with me so it would be better if he and I were partners instead. She seemed irate but agreed and stalked off with Brandon- who seemed pumped.

I felt bad for her. I knew how badly she wanted to repair their friendship. I just wish I knew why he didn't. I figured I would use this time on the way up to find out.

He wrapped his hand around my waist and led me into the seat. Is it ridiculous that I was swooning? We're just friends, we're just friends, we're just friends. Does repeating the same mantra over and over in your head make it true? If it did, my life would be a whole less messy. I decided it was now or never.

"What's on your mind, Aves? You have your detective face on."

"That easy to read, huh? Okay, it's about Macy."

"I thought we agreed last night to leave the past in the past."

"I know, but it's not about that. Macy isn't in the past. She's my friend. I THOUGHT she was yours too, but you don't seem interested in that. Why? You both made a mistake."

"Yeah, I thought we did too. The morning after though, she was going on and on about what a great couple we would be and that if I needed her to, she would be there to help me break the news to you."

"WHAT!?"

My head was spinning. This didn't make sense. After the incident, she made it a point to address it to everyone and emphasized clearly that it was a mistake she didn't intend on repeating. But now, Jason says she wanted them to be a couple. I don't know what to think. Is this why it's so awkward? I chalked the tension up to being the love triangle we unfortunately found ourselves in.

"Avery? You went quiet."

"Sorry, I'm trying to process. I didn't know she had feelings. She never said…"

"I know, and that's why I feel it better if her and I weren't friends. Look, sleeping with her was the worst mistake of my life and to hear she felt the opposite way made me look at her different."

I closed my eyes and leaned on Jason. My best friend had feelings for my boyfriend- well ex-boyfriend. Were they in the moment and fleeting or something that had been accumulating for a while? I didn't want to confront her on it, in fear that it would make our relationship even more strained than it already was- so I decided not to.

"Look Jason, can we keep this between us? I don't want to make it even more tense. And can you please make an effort to at least be cordial to Macy? Include her in the discussions, make eye contact, but please do something so that we can have a smooth weekend."

"Alright, I promise. Hey- you ready to go?"

I looked down and saw the biggest slope I had ever seen. A normal person would have been scared. Me? No, my adrenaline was pumping, and I just knew I was going to wipe the floor with Jason.

The attendant said his coveted, "Get ready…"

And just like that- we were off.

# **Chapter 3**

I started off at a great pace and was feeling confident. Of course, all of that went right out the window when I turned my head and saw that Jason was right on my tail. I curved a little to the right, and then to the left as an attempt at building my speed. He seamlessly mimicked my movements and increased his speed as well. Soon we were two clouds of fast movement zooming back and forth in a zigzag pattern each trying to overpass the other. I caught a break, and Jason's skis caught a twig and he fell. I guess I should thank the poor slope care from the Ski Resort, but I am going to put this all on my clearly exceptional skiing skills.

I skidded to a stop and helped Jason up. I am a good sport, after all. We were close to the bottom so just took off our skis and walked to meet our impatiently waiting friends. They had all seen Jason fall, and were doubled over with laughter. Brandon had tears in his eyes from cry-laughing so hard.

"Sorry to see you fall so hard there Jason. It happens to every beginner at some point," I winked.

"Please!! I had you until that point- you have to admit," he fired back.

"Yeah? Let's ask the judges, shall we?" and turned to my friends for their support.

Macy was the first one to jump to my defense noting that I was indeed the superior skier. Jason mumbled something about, "taking sides", and followed the rest of the group to the café at the bottom of the slopes. We entered the brightly lit café which had the most decadent arabica coffee bean scent. My favorite.

I could probably drink about a gallon of coffee a day, if it wouldn't kill me honestly. I do favor iced, but in weather like this I would kill for a steaming cup of hot coffee. The only person I knew to like coffee as much I did, was Macy. In fact, we have been hooked on the stuff since finals in 9th grade.

We swear to this day that it was the reason behind us being so successful and being able to cram the information from a whole school year into one night.

I was going to go up and order and turned to ask Macy what she wanted but saw her and Jason talking in the corner. I smiled. I'm glad they were finally clearing the air about what happened. Our friendship as a whole is so important to me, that I would hate to have anyone feel isolated or left out. If Jason and I can put the past behind us and strive for a healthy friendship, then him and Macy will be just fine.

I glanced over again, and they were both laughing and hugging it out. Brandon came over and looked as well, and chuckled, "Well that takes care of everything now. I take it you and Jason are good? You guys seemed exceptionally happy this morning. Did something happen last night?"

Ah, my ever-perceptive friend. "Yeah, we talked. We're friends, I want to move forward."

"I'm proud of you Aves, you're a lot stronger than me."

I hugged my friend and then ordered my medium coffee with two extra shots of espresso, black and a caramel macchiato for Macy.

"Damn Avery, I see you haven't lost your taste for the strong stuff," Jason said with a giggle.

"Hey, if I remember correctly you used to take it this way as well. Or have you lost your taste for it the same way you lost your ability to ski?" I teased.

He leaned close, and whispered, "I haven't lost my taste for a lot of things… but you already know that. Don't you?" and with that being said, sauntered away with a big grin on his face.

I joined the group and handed Macy her sugar laced caffeine. She gave me a small smile and leaned over, "Thanks for what you did. I know you put Jason up to talking to me. We worked it out, and we're friends. It's all thanks to you, Aves. You're the glue that keeps us all together."

"Of course. You guys are so important to me. I'm so grateful that everything is worked out."

"ENOUGH WHISPERING. Are we moving the party to the house or WHAT?"

"BRANDON!" we all scolded in unison.

Honestly, he was going to need to learn how to project a soft inside voice. We all loaded into Brandon's car and I sat in the front because Erica and Joey were sitting together practically having sex with their clothes on. I can live without hearing those noises for the rest of my life and be a happy girl. I was glad that my best friend finally was open about the way he felt for her. I was even more happy that she seemed to show a clear interest in him. Joey was a nice guy, and he deserved a great girl. I truly felt that if they gave their relationship an honest go, that they could still be standing in the end.

We pulled into the driveway of the familiar beautiful house and started unloading all of our ski equipment. Brandon's dad was really into the sport and had tons in his garage saving us money on renting the skis.

We all wanted to shower and given the fact that there was only one in the whole house- we enlisted a waiting list. To no one's surprise, Erica was first. She claimed if she didn't wash the snow out of her hair that it would frizz up. Yeah, I know, it didn't make sense to me either.

I was last, and so decided a walk would be fun. Jason, in a twist of events, opted to join me. We stepped outside and were immediately greeted with the cool and calming breeze. I started talking first.

"So… I heard you and Macy worked everything out. How do you feel?"

"Honestly Aves, good. I was fearful that she would want something I just couldn't give her, but she even admitted that she only said the things she did because she felt that our transgressions would cost her your friendship as well as everyone else's. "

"So, she felt you were all she had left. I get that. I would hope she knew we had been through way too much together for me to ever allow that to happen, but I do understand."

"I have a question for you though, and I apologize in advance if it sounds forward."

"Shoot. I seem to be all about being forward this trip so let's hear it."

"In the future, when all of this is long forgotten, do you suppose we could ever reconcile the romantic part of us? You are the only girl I have ever loved with my entire heart, and I hate to think that is irreparable."

I continued walking carrying a long silence with us. Truth is, I had thought about Jason and I getting back together. I would be lying to myself I had said I didn't think about it every day. However, while I forgive him- I don't know if I can fully trust him again. What if we were to break up again, and ruin our friendship with each other and everyone else to the point of no repair? My head was spinning.

"Aves…"

"Sorry. Well, in the spirit of full disclosure- I have thought about it. I have a lack of trust when it comes to you and me Jason. I'm fearful of us not being able to make it work and ruining this wonderful friendship we have. I can't imagine you not in my life."

"What if we took it slow? I promise you Avery, there will not be a point in time that you and I are no longer in each other's lives."

We smiled and hugged each other fiercely. I truly loved Jason with all my heart, and the words he spoke in the moment called to my soul and cracked open my heart that felt it had been closed to him indefinitely. He grasped the bottom of my chin and tilted my head up. One look in his sparkling eyes, and I caved.

Suddenly, we were kissing with so much passion and angst, and couldn't keep our hands off of each other. I grasped at his hair and tugged, he squeezed my waist and lifted me up. This time, it was Jason who broke away and said,

"Slow. Let's take this slow. I don't want to mess up again."

I smiled, grabbed his cold hand and started back up towards the cabin. When we arrived, I could smell Joey's famous chili on the stovetop. Everyone was showered and changed into comfy clothes surrounding the beautifully lit fire.

"I guess it's my turn to shower," Jason said and bounded up the stairs.

I headed towards my group of friends and was met with curious eyes and knowing smiles. Macy stifled a giggle and got up to pull me to the side.

"I see you have worked everything out with Jason as well. Any chance I get to see my two favorite people happy again?"

"Macy, I am happy, and I don't have to be with Jason to feel whole."

"I didn't say you weren't whole… that was you. You think we have been friends all these years and I don't know how to read you? C'mon," she said with a beaming smile that stretched ear to ear.

I sighed. I wanted more than anything to be with him again. It had been 7 months since what happened with Jason and Macy. If they could move on and be friends, and I could continue to be friends with both of them then what was stopping me from pursuing Jason romantically? Nothing.

I smiled at my best friend and ran up the stairs to meet a very wet Jason emerging from the shower.

"Avery, what are you doing?"

I pulled his towel off and we started kissing. Before I knew it, the familiar fire was burning again, coursing throughout my entire body. My skin felt hot and burned at his touch. This felt right… WE were right.

We pulled ourselves into his room and locked the door. He grabbed me and lifted me on top of his waist as he laid down. We stopped ourselves long enough for Jason to remind me we wanted to go slow.

"Jason, I know what we said but I feel for us to truly go after this then we should dive in the deep end. What do we have to lose?"

That's all it took for his lips to rejoin mine. He pulled my hair exposing my neck and trailing kisses all over. I couldn't take it anymore and started pulling off my wet clothes. I leaned back down and let my body take over.

We laid there in peaceful bliss for what felt like hours after. I knew everyone was probably downstairs waiting for us, and more likely than not knew exactly what was taking up our time. I reminded Jason I had to shower still, and against my will pulled myself out from his warm embrace. We shared a chaste kiss and with that I pulled back on my clothes and headed into the shower. The minute the hot water hit my sore muscles I was able to unwind after the puzzling day.

I loved hot showers that scalded my skin, and left my skin feeling raw after. I was always told by Jason how crazy I was for… and I quote, "taking showers that were hotter than the Devil's bath water." If anyone knows what in the hell that means, then by all means let me know. Jason was always saying weird things like that, sayings that only made sense to him and would have him doubling over in laughter after reciting them. I chuckled to myself. He really made me happy. Hopefully we could work this time.

I shut off the water and stepped out to grab a towel. I always needed two- one for my hair and one for my body. It's a girl thing, okay? I quickly dressed, and it was only then when I realized how starved I was. Having only coffee in your system all day will do that to you unfortunately.

I padded downstairs and was immediately greeted by the warm fireplace, the smell of chili, and my friend's laughter booming from the living room. I opened up the mahogany colored cabinet and pulled out the biggest bowl I could find and poured a generous helping of chili.

I wandered out to the living room to be greeted with, "Hey Aves, nice of you to join us. We were just asking Jason what took so long and how it took the amount of time for all of us to shower for you guys to take two. Or was it one?" Brandon said as he doubled over consumed with laughter. He thought he was hilarious.

My other friends must have thought so as well, including Jason, because they all joined in. I couldn't help but smile. Nothing was ever weird with all of us. We made fun of each other in the most lighthearted of ways and were thick as thieves. As I took a seat next to Jason, I feasted on Joey's chili.

"One day Joey you WILL give me this recipe… this is killer!" I boasted to my friend.

"Some day Aves, but for now- it's over my dead body," he smiled.

I could cook recipes perfectly, but Joey was different. With his dad owning the same grocery store for years, he learned how to create recipes from scratch. He was extremely creative and could come up with a random combination of food that seemingly always tasted like it was professional. Erica was in for a treat.

They had since moved on from our previous night's games and turned to a new one. Truth or drink. The rules? One person would announce something they had never done, and if you had- drink. It is a pretty exciting way to get drunk easily and quickly.

I skipped on the first round, because I was too infatuated with my dinner. Jason also sat out, because he had never been much a drinker and even less so since the incident. He didn't enjoy the idea of being intoxicated to the point of having no control over decisions. I can't lie, that made me feel appreciative. Jason was really trying.

Cue round one, and Erica went first.
"Never have I ever… gotten so drunk I fell asleep in a bathtub."

And just like that Brandon AND Joey raised their cups and drank, both objecting that it was one time. Joey decided to go next- "Never have I ever slept with someone in this group."

Macy drank, and Jason and I just looked at each other. Joey sensed the tension and immediately threw an apologetic glance towards my way. I couldn't blame him, that was Joey. He rarely thought his next sentence through until it was already on the tip of his tongue.

Needless to say, the vibe was awkward from then on out. Macy barely spoke, only drank. I couldn't blame her. I know she still feels like she is ostracized for her mistakes, but in reality, that couldn't be further from the truth. Macy always had been really down on herself, and that was one thing I always tried to get her to stop doing. She was a hilarious person who loved animals, nature, and making people happy. She was similar to Brandon in the sense that she was able to make people laugh naturally and lit up the room around her. However, the Macy I had seen for the past seven months was withdrawn and seemed as if the spark which used to light up her face was put out.

Maybe I underestimated how easy moving on would be. Maybe for Macy, she would never be able to. I shook away the negative thoughts and snapped back to reality. Apparently, it was my turn now.

"Never have I ever…took pictures of the midterms to pass Geometry." I said with a slight smirk directed at Joey.

Just like that, he tipped his cup back and took a big swig. He looked at me and I just shrugged. I figured I owed him one after the dig at Macy, or the unintentional dig at Macy… I don't know at this point. The game continued for several hours until everyone besides Jason and me were smashed, and about another sip from throwing up the contents of Joey's famous chili.

It only took about thirty more minutes before everyone was passed out, except for Jason and I- once again. Being the neat freak, I am, I started to collect all the solo cups, and bowls and brought them to kitchen. I set everything down and turned to get another batch when Jason came in carrying the rest.

"Thanks. I forgot how nice it is to NOT be completely wasted."
He laughed. "Not me, I don't ever miss it. I'd rather be completely in control of my actions. Plus, waking up with no hangover is an obvious bonus."
"Yeah, I can definitely see that. I wash, you dry?"
"Sure," and he reached out and grabbed the dish towel.

I have to say with the help, the cleanup went much quicker. Once the kitchen was fully cleaned, and all the trash was picked up and disposed of, I went to the living room to check on my friends. They were all peacefully sleeping, so I decided to lay a blanket on them and head up to bed.

My muscles were incredibly sore from the day of skiing. I hadn't been skiing in what felt like ages, and apparently my body felt the same way. I pulled back the covers of my bed, gave a once over to check for cockroaches, and laid down. I must have been out within the minute.

Morning came, and I didn't hear everyone talking downstairs this time. I rolled over and checked my phone… 9:27 am. Yeah, I was pretty positive my friends were still passed out or nursing their hangover with a cup of coffee.

I brushed my teeth and pulled my hair out of my face into a bun, and glided downstairs. Jason was right, no hangover in the morning is awesome.

I easily spotted everyone, and sure enough I was right. I could smell a fresh pot of coffee and beelined for the mugs. Once I took my first sip and felt human, I went and sat next to Macy. I grabbed her hand and dropped two Advil Migraine into it. She looked at her hand, at me, and whispered,
"You're a lifesaver."

I chuckled and continued my cup of coffee and noticed how close Erica and Joey had become. I couldn't help but feel warm inside at the thought of my best friend finally achieving the happiness he so desperately deserved. Brandon was playing on his switch his mom had gotten him as an early Christmas gift. I don't think he had put it down ten times since he first received it weeks ago.

The only person missing was Jason. I decided to go look for him and found him emerging from the guys bedroom with Brandon's keys and his wallet.
"Hey Aves. Sleep well?"
"I actually did. Who knew that having no skeletons in the closet would make for an *almost* sober night?" I smiled.
"Well it's no secret that you're better than the rest of us," and grabbed my hand and squeezed.

To my surprise, I found myself squeezing back and pulling him in for a hug. I still forget how good it feels to be next to Jason. He's always made me feel good about myself and builds me up to feel like I can conquer the world if I wanted to.

He told me that he asked Brandon if he could borrow the car to stop by the store and pick up a cake for tonight with sparkling apple cider. I almost forgot. Our yearly tradition. For the past couple of years, we would always take a trip somewhere a few weeks before Christmas, and our last night would always be complete with a decadent chocolate cake and washed down with apple cider. It's a weird combination, I know, but it's us.

I couldn't help but smile and found myself asking if I could accompany him on this "sacred tradition". He said yes, and I threw on my snowshoes and met him downstairs. I refilled Macy's drained coffee cup and told everyone to not have too much fun without me. They all smiled, or at least I think it was a smile. Honestly, they all looked like zombies this morning it was actually quite scary.

We got into the car and began to pick some songs to listen to as the car was warming up. Jason decided on, "Is It Enough" by Alex Roe. My heart melted into a puddle. He knew it was my favorite song, from my favorite movie- *Forever my Girl*. Maybe we had a shot after all.

He drove with one hand on the steering wheel as he always did, and his other hand found mine. He continued to do so the whole way until we arrived at Fisher's Grocery Market. Once inside, we searched high and low in the bakery to find the most over-the-top decadent gooey chocolate cake. We headed over to grab the cider and grabbed not one... but two bottles.

Jason insisted on paying, and I don't know why I found myself surprised as he had always done so while we were together. I finally ceded but with a stipulation- I carry the bags.

We loaded in the car and arrived back at the house quicker than usual. He had started acting weird all of a sudden. Before we went inside, I turned to him and demanded to know what was making him do a 360. He finally revealed that earlier the night before while I used the bathroom, Erica and Brandon got into a hushed heated discussion.

I was puzzled why that would bug him, considering those two were a cup or two away from blacking out. He started to fret and blurted out that he thought they might be sleeping together.

I tried to contain my laughter, but it was much too hard.
"Erica and Brandon?!? You're not being serious?"
"Yeah Aves, I am. I don't want anything else to drive a wedge in this group or ruin it the way Macy and I did."

It was my turn to console him,
"Jason, you and Macy didn't ruin anything. How many times do I need to reiterate this to the BOTH of you? You guys made a mistake."

He sighed and apologized for overthinking. I told him that Erica was pining over Joey from the minute they shared a kiss as part of a dare the first night. I also told him that I was pretty-positive that the argument was over something stupid, and that neither would've remembered this morning.

We decided to let it go, and finally grabbed the bags and headed inside.
"Hey, what took you two so long? If I don't have cake in my mouth within ten minutes...I just might die."

"I will applaud you for finally using an inside voice Brandon, but that can probably be chalked up to the massive hangover you're nursing right now. Can we please cut the dramatics? Let's have lunch first. I'm cooking."

With that, and Brandon's hushed mumbling about how his stomach was growling- I got to work. Today's lunch menu would be one of my most coveted recipes, fajitas. I got to work slicing the beef and threw it in the sauté pan complete with bell peppers, and onions. I added a splash of oil and sprinkled an abundance of various seasonings over the top.

I then took the cheese out of the fridge, along with the salsa, sour cream, hot sauce, and tortillas. I started to warm the tortillas on the stove and layered them on a tray for easy access. Once the meat and peppers were done, I let the heathens know it was time to eat.

I would say that they came bolting in, but that was an understatement. The night after drinking is hard on the stomach, I guess. Once everyone assembled their plate with toppings and fajitas, it was the chef's turn to eat. I made three and joined my friends.

To no surprise, Brandon was already licking his plate clean and bounding into the kitchen for seconds… or thirds. We all reminisced over the past few days and our previous yearly trips.

We truly held all these memories we made in our hearts forever. To all of us, these trips were a symbol that through the year we had- we remained friends and close as ever. I think this year felt even more special, because we really had gone through a lot with Macy and Jason's scandal.

Truth is, when it first happened it really divided our friend group. Joey was disgusted with both, Erica was telling all of us how alcohol ruins inhibitions and we should forgive and forget, and Brandon claimed he wasn't on sides, but rather wanted his friends to be okay. It was a trying time, but this trip served as an example, or rather a reward for all the obstacles we faced and overcame.

Once everyone was done, I went in the kitchen to clean up. I started spooning the leftover fajita mixture into the Tupperware, when Macy started to help clean up. Her and I spent the next twenty minutes laughing while we washed the dishes while taking turns spraying water at the other when they weren't looking. In the middle of one of these water fights, I caught Jason peeking in at the kitchen door. He just smiled, winked, and returned to the living room.

"Hey Aves, thanks for this. I know that trips like this aren't easy, but you have always done your part to make sure they pull through. It means a lot."

I smiled at my best friend and pulled her into a warm soapy embrace.

"I wouldn't have it any other way Macy."

"Can I borrow your sweater? The one I love? I'm freezing."

"Of course," I smiled.

Once the kitchen was finished, her and I rejoined the group who were now sprawled out over the couches and chairs squabbling about which Netflix movie to watch. Considering it was our last night here, we wanted to make the most of it and spend the day relaxing at the house.

Erica finally decided on a rom com, after we decided it be best that everyone gets their turn at selecting a movie with no complaints from the others. Brandon's pick of *Terminator* followed, and Joey's selection of *A Walk to Remember* practically brought the room to tears. Macy decided to ramp up the mood with a little *Dumb and Dumber*, and Jason decided *Fast and Furious* was the perfect act to follow.

Last but not least, it was my turn. I grabbed the remote, pressed play, and smiled over at Jason as the opening sequence to *Forever my Girl* began to play. By the time the movie finished, it was around seven. We were all rightfully starved and decided to order pizza so Chef Avery could have a break from cooking and cleaning.

It took all of thirty minutes for the delivery man decked out in top grade snow boots showed up with two extra-large pepperoni pizzas, and a ham and pineapple specifically for Jason. Why anyone thought pineapple should be a pizza topping is truly beyond me. I paid the man and added in a generous tip considering my pizza was still piping hot in freezing weather.

We all ate slice after slice, indulging in the love and laughter that filled our beautiful mahogany cabin that had began to feel like home over the past few days. By the time we finished eating, Brandon decided we should break into the chocolate cake and apple cider.

I cut everyone a slice, poured them a glass, and we assembled around the table sitting criss cross. We each took a turn reminiscing over our favorite moment from the year and then we feasted on one of the richest, and softest chocolate cakes I had ever had. We all tossed back the disgusting apple cider, except for Joey who sipped on it slowly as if it was the finest Parisian wine.

It wasn't long before Brandon broke out Jack Daniels, or what I like to refer to as "Devils Juice". He insisted we all took shots, partial to only Jason. We continued until the bottle was finished. Erica and Joey had fallen asleep in each other's arms sprawled across the cozy loveseat. Brandon had made his way upstairs with the help of Jason and me. I helped Macy up the stairs into our bedroom and came back downstairs to resume the cleanup.

No shock here, but Jason wanted to lend a helping hand. He was always good like that, wanting to help where he felt it was needed. He expected nothing in return, because he had such a giving heart. A nasty little voice in the back of my head reminded me that he was maybe "too giving" and I flashed back to walking in on Macy and him asleep the morning after. I shook the image away and finished up on the kitchen.

We laid on the couch opposite Joey and Erica snoring peacefully and we talked for hours until we too, were peacefully snoring.

I woke up and the only one up was Joey. It was early morning, but we had needed to be checked out by 11 am. I decided to bite the bullet, and just get up. Joey was in his room packing alone. Weird. I wonder if Brandon made his way into Macy's room last night…

My thoughts were interrupted by a disheveled Macy sauntering into the room rubbing her eyes, "Morning guys."
"Hey Mace, you look like hell. How do you feel?"
"I'm assuming not better than I look," she said with a smile.

Her and I went into the room and started packing up the rest of our stuff. I started grilling her about Brandon and her, when she seemed confused.
"Why would I have been with Brandon? He was asleep in his room from what I thought. If you remember correctly, so was I."

I reminded her that I knew that but assumed because he obviously isn't in there with Joey now. I gave her a side hug and went downstairs to see what the rest of my friends were up to-hopefully packing as it was now 9:23 am.

Jason was all packed and was sipping on a hot cup of coffee as he stared out the window watching the snow fall, and Erica was indulging in a chocolate croissant. Jason turned around and greeted me with a smile when he saw me.

"Hey Aves, was Brandon packing? I know he likes to sleep in, but we have a checkout time looming," he said cracking a smile.

In that moment, I felt the strangest sense that something was horribly wrong. I let him know that Brandon wasn't upstairs and apparently, he wasn't downstairs either. So, where the hell was he? I yelled for Macy and Joey to meet us downstairs and we all discussed where he could have gone until Jason suggested we check for his car, and that maybe he went to the store for road snacks. I took the liberty of peeking outside and noticed that his car was gone.

We all breathed a sigh of relief until we noticed his wallet on the counter. I decided to check outside again, and nearly slipped on Macy's wet boots doing so. There was no sign of him.

We waited until 11 am for Brandon, but alas he was a no show. This was so unlike him, to run out without letting anyone know. I expressed my concerns to the group that something terrible might have happened to him. As we waited, we decided it best to call his mom and give her a heads up. She agreed that it was unlike him and started to panic. I began to talk her down and explained that we would continue to wait for as long as it takes and call her soon with an update. Erica started crying, Joey began to stress clean, and Macy was on the verge of a mental breakdown. We were all so worried about our friend, and I found Jason upstairs trying to track Brandon's phone with no luck. The hours began to tick on by with no reassurance. We gave an update to our house renter, and waited until 1 in the afternoon, when we decided to call the local police department.

"Hello, this is Gainespole Police Department. How can I assist you?"
 "It's my friend Brandon. He's missing."

# **Chapter 4**

Never in a million years did I think that I would be interviewed by the police about the disappearance of one of my best friends. The worst part is that last night was so fuzzy, I truly can't remember the last time I saw Brandon. I do know that Jason and I had to both help him up the stairs into his room and onto the bed. He was completely intoxicated.

The cops seem to think that he just wandered off in the midst of his drunken haze. It is infuriating, because I have a gut wrenching feeling that that is not the case, and something is horribly wrong. Brandon drank enough to put him in a coma, so there is absolutely no way in hell that he simply got up, grabbed his keys and drove off. My only comfort is in that I know he has the car, and the ability to stay warm… but for how long?

I had no time to worry about my friend, because we were being pulled in all different directions, and forced to answer every mind numbing and useless question they threw at us.

The cop questioned, "What type of alcohol did you guys drink?"

I couldn't take this anymore.

"Why the hell are you curious about what TYPE of alcohol we drank? One of our friends is MISSING AND STANDING AROUND ASKING USELESS QUESTIONS IS NOT GOING TO HELP FIND HIM," I bellowed.

The cop tried to reassure me that it was procedure, and they were doing all they could at the moment to find Brandon. Jason pulled me aside and embraced me in a hug. I couldn't help myself as I started to sob uncontrollably into his shoulder. He gently squeezed me and placed a kiss on my forehead.

"We will find him Aves. You know Brandon, he probably went to get Jack in the Box and just forgot where it was so pulled over and slept."

"Why haven't they found his car yet then?" I practically wailed. With that, he squeezed me again before another detective interrupted. They informed me that they had scoped within the immediate area out but were now expanding to a five-mile radius. Finally. I breathed a sigh of relief, as I felt that they were finally putting in effort to find my friend. Erica was being consoled by Joey, as they were both being interviewed pretty intensely by a Detective Greene. I marched over and demanded to know why we were all still being interviewed, as we had given all the information we had. Detective Greene reassured me that due to the amount of alcohol consumed last night, there may be new information that will start to come out during the day as we sober up.

He walked away, and I was left with my friends who couldn't have looked more terrified in that moment. Joey grabbed my hand and asked how I was doing.

"Well, our best friend is missing, they haven't found his car, or him for that matter, and all they've been doing is asking us the same damn questions for hours!"

Joey grabbed me and calmed me down by reminding me that like the police said, it's procedure. He also assured me that they were doing everything they could, and he had no worries that Brandon would be home safe and sound soon- probably ready for his next drink.

I couldn't help but laugh. Joey always knew how to keep me sane, and that was an asset in a situation like this. I don't know why I was so angry with the police officers. They were just trying to do their job. My friend was missing, I had no answers, no information, and I needed someone to be angry at. Although, I think the person I was truly upset with was myself for letting this happen.

At that moment, Detective Greene motioned for all of my friends for us to join him: a worried Jason, grief-stricken Macy, a calm but nervous Joey, a sobbing Erica, and me- the angry one. The detective was the first to speak.

"Like I said, we are expanding our investigation to search within a five-mile radius. We have taken all your statements and will be in touch if we find new information. Until then, please stay in the immediate area."

And with that, he turned and left. All of us started speaking a hundred miles a minute, until I asked Macy what she told the detectives.

"I told them all I can remember- which wasn't much. I was also really drunk, so I told them about the movies, the traditional cake and apple cider, then the shots that Brandon had ordered us to take. I also slightly remember Avery pulling me upstairs and putting me to bed."

That did sound about right. I was able to remember things a tad bit clearer than the others because after about two shots, I started to throw them over my shoulder into the plant. As a matter of fact, I should probably replace that...

My thoughts were interrupted by Joey inquiring about what I had told the police.

"Well it's pretty simple, I told them everything that happened last night. I was drinking but didn't feel drunk and explained the first half of the night as you did Mace. I told them that Jason and I both put Brandon to bed, and I helped Macy to hers. By the time we wrangled those two and got downstairs, Joey and Erica were passed out on the loveseat."

Jason added, "Then Avery and I decided to sleep on the couch as well."

It seemed that in terms of the night's events, we were all in agreeance on what had happened. The weirdest thing that I couldn't look past, is how did the most intoxicated of us all get up, get in the car, and drive to God knows where without any of us stirring? I wasn't drunk, but I know from experience that Jason and I are pretty heavy sleepers, especially when exhausted.

Something simply wasn't adding up. His phone was in his pocket when he left, as I remember feeling it when bang against my knee as I lifted his legs onto his bed. Leave it to Brandon to get the biggest phone on the market right now. Oh! That's a clue, right? I called up the number the detective left.

"Hello, this is Detective Greene speaking."

"Hi Detective, it's Avery. I thought of something else, but don't know if it is any use to you. Last night, as I was helping Brandon into bed, I felt his phone in his pocket. This morning, Jason tried to track it but was not able to. Maybe you'll have more luck?"

I gave Detective Greene the phone number, and he let me know he would update me after they tried to locate it.

I rejoined my friends with a little more pep in my step. I had hope. Little did I know that my hope would be instantly crushed when I answered my phone.

"Avery, it's Detective Greene. We tried to track the phone but had absolutely no signal. This means that the phone died or was deliberately turned off."

I felt my chest squeeze with disappointment before he added, "However, there is a good thing. We can now go search the area where the phone gave off it's last signal before going off. Apparently, it's about six miles east of you. Will update you later."

And with that, he hung up. I turned to my friends excitement clear on my face and explained what had happened. To my surprise, Macy was the only one not excited. She expressed that she was terrified that when they found Brandon, it wouldn't be good.
"I can't help but feel a pit in my stomach. Brandon was three times the legal limit allowed to drive. Why would he be six miles east of the house? What if he crashed?" she wailed.

I didn't see things that way until Macy did. Oh god, what is something horrible did happen to Brandon? What if he crashed? Did he lay there waiting for help for hours until his phone died? Oh god, what if he was dead? I was letting my worse thoughts take over when I was interrupted by Jason pulling me into the kitchen.
"Aves, I can see that you're scared. We can not let everyone else see that. We have to keep the hope that Brandon is safe and probably just asleep at the wheel of an idled or parked car. I know from experience what overthinking or letting your darkest thoughts take over can do."

I realized he was right, and that I had to keep faith that Brandon would be okay. As much I used to not think so, I felt the group had always looked to me in sort of a leadership role, and if I started to fall apart- they would too.

Okay, guys, let's not sit here and do nothing. I can't just be idle. Let's search for clues as to why Brandon may have left, and I'll call his mom and update her. She has to be freaking out right about now. She answered on the first ring, and I filled her in on everything that had happened this morning since calling the police. She felt relieved that they were in route to the phone, and hopefully the car and Brandon. I could tell she was still nervous about the scene they would find. Brandon's mother knew full well just how much Brandon loved to party and drink and couldn't fathom why he would knowingly get behind the wheel of a car following.

I let her know I would call with more information and clicked the phone. I turned to find my friends in all areas of the house examining the remnants of the night before. I knew that there would probably be nothing to find, considering it was pretty-straight forward. We knew Brandon was drunk, we knew we brought him to his room, and that at some point later in the night, he grabbed only his keys and left. He must not have been planning to be gone for very long, considering he didn't grab his wallet or let any of us know.

That begs the question… what was so important that Brandon felt he had to leave in the middle of the night?

My head was spinning. I decided I would move my search party outside. I thought that maybe, Brandon had dropped something outside that would give me some sort of clue or idea to where he would have gone. I saw the obvious tire tracks and noted the car had been heading East. It's wasn't much of a surprise, due to the fact that the detective already let me know that's where Brandon's phone gave off it's last signal. I tried to look at the footprints, but they had been completely worked over from the hoard of cops that had been filtering in and out of the house all morning.

I decided to put my sleuthing skills to rest and headed inside with hopes that my friends had better luck at uncovering clues then I had.

Unfortunately, their search had come to a standstill and they were all sitting in the living room once again trying to piece together the previous night's events. I bounded up the stairs and examined the boy's room once more. Brandon's sheets and blanket were completely disheveled. It was almost as if he had also left in a hurry. My thoughts were interrupted by the loud ringing of my cellphone. I checked the caller i.d.- Detective Greene. I answered immediately.

"Hello? Detective? Did you find anything?"
"Avery. Are you and your friends still at the house?" he said curtly.
"We are. What's going on?"
"Stay right where you all are. I am dropping by now," he said and hung up the phone abruptly.

What the hell? A sense of dread began to fill my entire body. It had to be bad. They must have found Brandon, and he was badly injured. He probably crashed his car. Oh god, he was probably in the hospital. I couldn't stop thinking of the worst thing to happen to him. Why did we let him drink so much? Why didn't I hear him leave? I could have helped him- WE could have all helped him.

I decided after ten minutes of stressing alone in the room, that I had to break what I thought would be bad news to my friends. Little did I know that it was going to be the worst news of our lives.

As I came downstairs and opened my mouth to speak, there was a loud bang on the door. I went to answer it and Detective Greene as well as four other policemen came charging in.

Before I could find the words to ask what they found, the detective cut me off.

"So, who's going to fess up?"

I was taken aback. Fess up? To what? We all started buzzing with confusion before Detective Greene added,

"We found the car… as well as Brandon's dead body in the backseat."

# **Chapter 5**

I couldn't believe what I was hearing. Brandon was dead. Someone killed him. Detective Greene thought that "someone" could be one of us.

Erica and Macy started sobbing. Joey looked broken, and Jason looked at me with tears in his eyes. I felt crushed. I felt like a piece of me died. I didn't know how to think or process any of it. I started to wonder how he died, if he suffered, and why it happened. I couldn't help but feel absolutely broken. That ache in my heart only worsened when I thought of Brandon's mom, and that someone had to tell her that her only child, her son, was murdered. That he would never return home, and never be around to tell her that her cooking was bad ever again. Oh god… what the hell happened?

There was no time to properly grieve for my friend, because the detectives starting to load us into the squad cars to take us down to the precinct for more questioning. They really thought we did it. These detectives felt that one of us was truly capable of this type of evil. We all loved Brandon. We didn't do it, we couldn't have.

We pulled into the precinct, were brought inside and immediately separated into different interrogation rooms. This was so surreal. I felt like these past 24 hours had been such a whirlwind of emotions, that I had no time to process or deal with. Now I know my friend is dead and never coming back, and I don't even have the time to properly grieve. Instead, I have to prove my innocence to these detectives who think that I could be capable of murdering Brandon.

Detective Greene entered the room. He had a somber look on his face. I mentally prepared myself to withstand whatever mind games he was prepared to play.

"Well Avery, you're in a lot of trouble. Your friends are in there with my detectives right now confessing about what you did."

I was momentarily stunned, until I realized what he was doing. I was an avid criminal justice fan and had watched enough shows to know that Detective Greene was trying to trick me into confessing to killing Brandon. I must admit he was doing a stellar job. It may have even actually worked... on someone who was guilty.

I simply stared at him. Was this how the investigation was really going to go? An endless cycle of pointed fingers from friend to friend, all while being fed lies by the police. I wished more than anything that I could erase last night. I wanted to go back in time to tell Brandon that he didn't need to drink, and instead filled his cup with more apple cider rather than Jack Daniels. My heart ached, and once again my thoughts were interrupted by Detective Greene. "Tell me something, Avery. Did you lift him into the backseat by yourself or was he already laying there when you bashed his brains in?"

I was sick to my stomach. Brandon was beat to death? I couldn't fathom the idea of someone having that much rage and hatred to bash his brains in- certainly not one of my friends and most definitely not me. I finally spoke.
"You're so obsessed with closing this case, that you are grasping at straws. None of my friends could have hurt Brandon, and I certainly didn't do it either. He was one of my best friends. This has to be a mistake."
"You're right about one thing, I do want to close this case. However, I do want to find the real killer, but it seems I already have."
"How could I have done that when I was asleep next to Jason the entire night? What exactly do you think I did? Woke up, got Brandon into the car, drove him six miles away and killed him? What do I possibly have to gain from that?"
"See that's what I'm trying to figure out as well. Maybe you had a drunken disagreement that turned violent. Maybe you were just defending yourself. Point is, I can't help you unless you tell me the truth."

I put my head in my hands. I was getting no where with him. How many ways could I explain the truth, that I didn't do it. He would never believe I was innocent until they caught the real killer. So, who did it? It couldn't have been Jason, as he was next to me until morning. Macy was completely comatose upstairs, and Joey and Erica were asleep on the loveseat. That settled it. None of us could have done it. I looked up just as Detective Greene left the room.

I was left alone to drown in my own thoughts. As much as I tried to solve this in my head, I couldn't. I didn't have all the facts. I only knew as much as I had been told or remembered. Maybe Brandon went outside to find something and had been mugged by some lowlife. Maybe that guy drove him away and killed him. His wallet was on the counter, so that wouldn't have made sense. God, this was too much for me to process and my head was spinning.

It felt like hours before the door finally opened again, and in walked a new detective. He smiled and handed me a cup of coffee. Great, they sent in "good cop". Nevertheless, these anticipated tactics wouldn't work. Eventually they would get bored with the same truth I would continue to give them. Hopefully then they would start to look for the actual killer instead of mercilessly pursuing my friends and me.

He took a seat and continued what I think he believe to be his "kind smile". I really wish he'd stop. It was beginning to remind me of the clown from IT.

"Avery, we're just trying to help. If you tell me the truth, I can help you. If it was one of your friends, you don't need to cover for them."

I had to stop my eyes from rolling to the back of my head. How dense could these guys be? I could continue to tell them that none of us did it, we all loved Brandon, and that this was a mistake. They didn't believe that version, as they seemingly already created an alternate one of their own. This was pointless. I decided to just stay silent- it was my right after all.

The detective decided to stay with me, probably grasping at some fleeting sense of hope that I would break down and confess. I had nothing to confess to, so we sat. The time passed so slowly, that by the time he finally gave up it had felt like the day was over. I wouldn't know, as they kept me in this ten by ten brick room with no windows and only one clear pane that allowed me to look back at myself. I knew well enough that it was see through on only one end-theirs.

Finally, a familiar face popped their head in. Mom. I got up and sprinted over to give her a hug. I don't think I had ever been so ecstatic to see someone in my life. My mom was nothing but warm smiles, and kindness. This room I had been kept in felt like the complete opposite.

"Ready to get out of here Avery?"

"You have no idea. They're letting me go?"

She smiled. "Of course, they are, they have no evidence. Plus, I don't think they feel that you actually did it."

"If you had been in here an hour ago, you would have been surprised."

She just squeezed my side, and together walked out. When I emerged, I saw all my friends and their parents sitting in the waiting area… as well as Brandon's mom who was sobbing uncontrollably. My heart broke for her. I beelined for her and embraced her in a tight hug, but to my surprise she pushed me away- hard.

"You killed my baby!" she growled with menace.

"What? No, I would never! Brandon was family to us!"

She practically lunged at me dripping with hatred before one of the uniformed policemen took her away. My jaw probably hit the floor right about now. I looked up at my friends with wide eyes, and they all shared the same expression. Not only did all of the detectives believe we were capable of such violence, so did Brandon's mom. When would this nightmare end?

Before I could begin to think of an answer to that question, Detective Greene strolled over to us. He looked pinched and handed all of us his card with a number listed.

"Look, you're all able to go… for now. Here is my card and number if you think of anything else. You're able to go home, but I wouldn't go too far."

With that, he turned and stalked away. I found Jason and asked him to call me when he got home and planted a soft kiss on his cheek. He squeezed my hand as he walked away letting me know, it was okay. I said my goodbyes to Joey, Erica, and let Macy know I would text her when I got home. She returned a meek smile and said okay.

My mom grabbed my shoulder lightly acknowledging it was time to head home. I began to walk out with her when I felt someone staring. I turned around to find Detective Greene standing in the doorway of his office- watching me. He gave a slick nod and retreated into the office.

This man was delusional. Right off the bat, he doesn't give us any time to actually process our friend's murder. He immediately separates us into different rooms, and hurls questions at us, messing with our already fragile mental state.

I found myself pushing the hard as nails detective to the back of my mind and focused in Brandon. I couldn't imagine a day where I would miss his obnoxiously loud voice. At this moment in time, I found comfort in it. I would do anything to hear it again, one last time. My mom reached out and gave me a comforting smile. I loved how supportive she was. She didn't get it though, and the only ones who did were in different cars.

I decided to send out a group message: Meet at Graham Park at six tonight. We all need to talk.

It wasn't long after that when I began to receive replies left and right.

Jason: See you there Aves.

Macy: Of course.

Joey: I'll be there.

Erica: Got you. See you all later- xo.

I sighed and breathed out the tiniest bit of relief since the cops broke the news and hauled us into the station. I knew if I ever needed it that my mom would be there with an endless shoulder to cry on, and an ear that would never stop listening. But, something of this degree needed people around that actually were there. They all went through the motions with me: realizing Brandon was missing, searching for any clue, hearing he not only died but he was murdered, and being questioned. I'm sure everyone can only imagine how much that is for someone to go through in two days and my friends didn't have to imagine. They felt the same way.

We pulled into our familiar driveway, and I must admit that seeing our big brick house brought me a sense of comfort. I was home, in my safe space where no one could hurt me. Wait, where did that come from? I didn't fear for my life… did I?

If I am going for complete disclosure, a part of me is frightened. I don't feel as if I am in immediate danger or anything. If someone as kind and warm hearted as Brandon can be murdered as brutally as he was, what's to stop the killer from coming after me next? It's hard to calm that small voice in my head, especially since we don't even know why he was murdered. How could we, since the police have ditched the idea of it being an outside killer but rather someone from my small group of friends?

Instead of continually trying to solve this in my head, I opted to save all my questions for when I see my friends. Bouncing ideas off of them should help me reach a conclusion. I put my bag down in my room and headed straight for the shower. The hot water should bring me some clarity or at least clear my head.

I turned on the shower all the way to the only acceptable temperature- scalding. I stepped in and let the water cascade down my head. In no time, I was enveloped in steam and physically felt my muscles relax. If only hot water could solve the tension in my head as well. I was in there for about ten minutes, and after fulling getting clean, I stepped out and dried off. I looked in the mirror, and almost didn't recognize the person staring back at me. I had dark purplish circles under my eyes, as if I hadn't sleep in a week. Despite being in a boiling shower, my skin was pale and sallow.

I decided that nitpicking myself after a long day wouldn't make me feel any better about Brandon. I got dressed in a warm cream sweater, and some leggings. I brushed my hair out, added a little concealer for my eyes, threw on my boots and headed downstairs.

"Where are you going Avery? It's nearly dinner time." My mom scolded.

"I'm meeting the group at Graham Park. We haven't had a chance to properly talk since… you know."

She gave a sad smile and nodded, letting me know that was fine. I stepped outside and checked my phone- 5:46. I lived about a five-minute walking distance from the park, so I took my time. Usually I would love the cold air, but after this weekend I seemed to have lost my edge for all things cold. I popped in my headphones and cranked the volume all the way up as a means of distraction- anything to stop thinking about Brandon.

It wasn't long before I reached the entrance of the park. It wasn't gated, so I could see clear across the widespread mound of grass. I easily spotted my friends already gathered around the picnic benches- our usual meeting spot. Usually when we would meet up, there was laughter and lightheartedness in the air. Now, the mood was somber, and everyone matched with purplish bags and tear rimmed eyes.

I went straight for my best friend Macy who looked completely destroyed. We embraced in the longest hugs I think we ever had had. Macy was never a touchy-feely kind of person, and I respected that. Right now, I think we all just desperately sought a mutual comfort from one another.

I reached my hand out to Jason, and he took it. I was so glad that we had patched things up because if some of us were still on the outs with each other, this whole situation would have been harder to cope with. In a way, it helps slightly that we are so tight knit. I glanced over at Joey who began to sob. Erica grabbed him and pulled him in an embrace and began to cry as well. I beelined for those two and wrapped my arms around both. It wasn't long before I too began to cry.

We sat there holding each other and crying until we ran out of tears. We sat down and fell into a comfortable silence. Jason's hand found mine once more. I was the first to speak.
"We haven't had a chance to talk about what happened to Brandon. It all happened so fast."
Jason said, "I know. Can you believe they actually think we did it?"

We all shook our heads. We knew there was not a chance either of us did it. I was glad in this moment for our sense of unity. Something like this usually can rock friendships, and even break trust but not us. We were solid, and always had been.
Joey began to speak. "Did they tell you how he died? They wouldn't tell me but kept insisting I already knew."

I went pale as I said, "Detective Greene said his brains were bashed in."

The entire group fell into a silence. Macy looked like she was going to throw up, and everyone had turned pale. I understood it. When Detective Greene broke the news to me in a rather blunt way, and I found myself sick to my stomach. You don't ever want to have anything horrible happen to your friends, and I feel extremely grateful that the police found him like that and not one of us. I don't think I would have been able to ever sleep again if I saw Brandon in that state.

"Has anyone talked to Brandon's mom since the police station?" Erica added.

We all shook our heads no almost on cue. I can't believe that she thought we did it- that *I* did it. I was there on birthdays, holidays, and even one time that I got in a horrible fight with my mom. It was like I told her at the station, we were a family. I don't think any one of my friends had a mean bone in their body, certainly not one of this level. Brandon was the light in our group, bringing sunshine and laughter to even the darkest of times. He knew how to turn the mood around instantly. He was someone you could never be mad at.

I looked around at my friends. "If the cops aren't going to try and find his actual killer, I say we do it."

Everyone looked taken aback. Their responses were all the same as if they had been reading from a cue card. I should have known that they didn't want to investigate on our own. They all decided that while it really sucked that the police were looking at us, they would lose focus of that when they saw that there was no evidence. They wanted me to leave the dirty work and investigating to the police. Not wanting to have a disagreement, I just went along with what they said and left it at that.

Just then my phone rang, and it was my mom asking me to return home. It had gotten dark, and I knew she was still on edge from Brandon's murder. I let my friends know, and Jason offered to walk me home. I agreed and said goodbye to all my friends.

We took each other's hands and began to walk under the light of streetlamps. He took his thumb and grazed it over my knuckles. We continued our walk, relishing in the comfortable silence and the other's company. It alleviated all my worries to have the reassurance that I didn't have to go through this alone. Once we reached my house, he pulled me into an embrace, and kissed me gently. He told me to text him anytime- that he would be there for me. I smiled at Jason and let myself into the house.
"How was it? Do you feel better after talking to your friends?"
This time I faked a smile and said, "I really do. Thanks for everything mom."

I turned and headed upstairs to my room. Once the door was closed, I erupted into a fit of tears. I wasn't okay, how could I ever be? Apart of me was happy for the support, but they were uninterested in trying to search for Brandon's killer ourselves. I wiped my tears away and pulled out my laptop. I pulled up a car rental service and set a time to be picked up tomorrow. I typed in my destination address and closed my laptop.

If they weren't going to help me find Brandon's killer, then I would do it myself.

# **Chapter 6**

I woke up to my phone's alarm chiming. I silenced it and pulled myself out from the warmth of my blanket. I had my clothes already set out and ready from the night before, so I quickly dressed myself. I made sure I had everything- phone, keys, and wallet. I checked the time- 3:15 a.m. The car would be here in ten minutes to pick me up. I wanted to be out before my mom got up for work, and noticed I was missing.

I waited outside for the car to pull up. Right on cue, a silver Nissan came into sight. The driver didn't have any time to park before I climbed into the backseat and fastened my seatbelt. He turned around and smiled.

"So, we're heading to 874 Brightbear Lane? Going skiing huh?"

"Something like that."

He chuckled and started on his way. The scenery as we transitioned into the mountains was breathtaking. You could see the snow covering the mountains, and the roads were cleared. You always knew you were almost to the snow resort area because you passed by at least ten hand carved bear statues. By the time we had almost arrived, the sun was starting to come up and shine. My phone buzzed with a text from my mom: Where are you?

I responded: Went to Macy's to sleepover. Was upset.

She didn't want to push so just send back a quick: Okay, I love you.

I hated lying to her, but I simply wasn't like the rest of them. I couldn't just continue with my life, while Brandon's real killer remained free. No, that person would pay for what they did. I would make sure of it.

The driver pulled up in front of the all too familiar mahogany home. I thanked the driver, paid him, and let him know I would call when I would be ready to leave. Once I stepped out of the car, the all too familiar feeling of nausea came rushing over me. I played through the weekend's events in my head. Arriving, skiing, Joey's chili, the traditional cake, fun drinking games, and then the cops.

I had texted the homeowner on the way over here and asked if she would leave a key. I told her I had forgotten my charger under the bed. When did I develop a knack for lying? I lifted the welcome mat and found the spare key. I unlocked the door as slowly as I could, and stepped in.

The sense of dread that filled my entire body was unwelcoming. Everything looked the same as how we'd left it, except with a very pungent lemon cleaner odor. The place had been wiped from head to toe. According to the owner, she was now closing her home from being rented to young adults. She complained that the cops made such a mess searching for evidence, that it took her a whole day to clean it. I was going to add that I went home with one less friend than I arrived with, but I guess her problems are important too.

If the cops were done searching, then they must have taken all worthy evidence with them. There was surely nothing here. That wasn't going to stop me from looking though. I was nothing if not stubborn. I headed upstairs to check the boy's bedroom first. All the beds were neatly made, and freshly vacuumed. I sighed in frustration. If there was anything of importance, it was long gone.

I did a quick peek in the girl's room and found the same scene. Freshly cleaned, with fresh sheets and a vacuumed floor. I was feeling pretty defeated but decided to take a look around the downstairs floor. Everything was spot clean… shocker. Damn it. I wish I knew where the scene of the crime was so I could check it out, but figured it would be similar to the house- any evidence found would be in the police's custody.

I decided to cut my losses and began to head outside when I nearly ran into the homeowner, Lisa.
"Did you find your charger?"

I was taken aback, and with no charger in sight, faked a sigh and said, "No, but it's okay. I'll just buy a new one."

She didn't look convinced but didn't question any further. I handed her the key and she went to open the door. Before she retreated inside she turned around and said,

"I'm sorry about your friend. I think it would be better if you and your friends didn't return here. Let the other girl know too."

I was obviously taken aback by the last comment when she began to elaborate further.

"Your friend, Lacy or Kacey whatever her name was. I found her here late last night looking around the front of the house in a panic. I'll tell you the same thing I told her- leave it to the cops."

She went into the house and shut the door. I was reeling from her revelation. Macy was here? Why? When I mentioned the idea of trying to look for clues in Brandon's death, she shut down and dismissed the idea swiftly. The rest of my friends did the same, but the others didn't come here late last night alone either. I needed answers, but I wasn't going to find them here. I didn't want to upset Lisa any further, so I decided to walk a little bit and hopefully work some of this out in my head.

What if Macy decided to come alone, as I had? Wouldn't she rather of agreed with my plan yesterday and joined me? Two pairs of eyes were better than one, and I felt hurt that she didn't think I was worthy of being a good accomplice. Maybe she was being classic Macy and didn't want me to get in trouble. She was like that. Macy was always selfless and rarely put herself before others.

Still, it doesn't change the fact that she lied. However, I can't exactly call myself the poster girl for truth especially lately. Lying to my friends, lying to my mom, what was I trying to accomplish?

I brushed off the nagging voice of my head, and reminded myself that all the lies, and the sneaking around was serving a purpose. I was going to find Brandon's killer. I didn't care how long it took.

"A little far from home, are we?"

I knew that voice anywhere. I turned around.

"Hello Detective Greene. What are you doing here?"

"Funny. I was going to ask you the same thing. Come here to destroy evidence have we?"

God, this man was dense.

"I actually came here to find any clues that would lead to the discovery of Brandon's killer. I hoped that they weren't careful and left something of importance behind. It seems that your precinct took everything though."

He looked thoughtful for a minute, as if he was actually considering the possibility that I wasn't the killer, and that my intentions were genuinely pure. The moment was fleeting, and he returned to his coveted "bad cop" role.

"Or maybe… you came here because the guilt has become too much. How about you come down to the precinct with me and confess?"

I started to become angry. To be telling the whole truth, and constantly be called a liar, and to have your character questioned is so damn frustrating. I was tired of playing this stupid cat and mouse game with Detective Greene.

"Unless I'm under arrest which would be impossible since I didn't do anything, then I'm going home. I hope that you and your department decide to pull your heads out of your asses and focus on the real killer. Tell me something, do you wake up this stupid or is it something you have to strive towards?"

I had a lot more to say but was interrupted by the feel of cool metal cuffs being slapped on my wrist.

"Avery Grant, you're under arrest for disturbing the peace."

Just like that, he began to read me my rights. Disturbing the peace? I didn't realize that calling a detective stupid, rightfully so, would be an arrestable offense. So much for keeping my rendezvous trip here secret.

He pushed the top of my head low and lowered me into the backseat of his car. I couldn't believe this. First, my friend is murdered and I'm a suspect. Second, I come here only to find no clues, and get into a verbal war with one very angry detective- at least now he is.

We rode in silence on the way to the precinct. Why did I think it would be a good idea to call a detective stupid? Especially one that is investigating my friend's murder… maybe I was the stupid one.

I decided that if I wanted the true killer to be caught, that I needed the cops on my side. They needed to see the real Avery Grant, and that I was not a killer but that someone out there was.

"I'm sorry Detective Greene. This whole thing has been a whirlwind of emotions for not only my friends and I, but our families. I miss Brandon more than I can put into words." I said with a tear beginning to roll down my cheek.

I nestled my face into my shoulder to wipe the tears away. I wouldn't let him see me cry. It was too late, because I looked up and caught the detective staring at me in the rearview mirror with a sympathetic look plastered all over his face.

Just like that, he pulled his car over to the side of the road. He put the car in park, unbuckled his seatbelt and turned around. "Avery, I really am trying to do my job. However, you guys are prime suspects. Until I find a piece of evidence that rules you all out, that's the hard truth."

I considered what he said for a moment. I wondered if he would allow me to take a look at the evidence they did collect, if any. Maybe my eyes would allow me to help draw a conclusion to who Brandon's murderer was, or why they did it. I still refused to believe it was one of my friends.

I propositioned Detective Greene with my idea, and he stewed on it for a minute. He decided that it would be fine, and that maybe I would be able to shed some light on things.

We started back on our way to the precinct, after he removed the hard handcuffs and allowed me to move to the front seat. I had a feeling that he didn't think of me as a suspect anymore. Problem is, he still had an inkling that one of my friend's did it. I had hopes that whatever evidence they had in custody would be successful in clearing my friend's names.

We arrived at the precinct and went into one of the interrogation rooms. The detective and I sat down opposite one another. He started by filling me in on what they do know. They know Brandon was murdered, that's a given. They also know that the steering wheel was wiping clean, and there was not a single fingerprint. If anyone had driven the car, there would have been. Apparently, this led them to believe that Brandon didn't drive the car to the location they found it. If he did, there would be no reason for the steering wheel to be wiped clean. The murderer drove it at some point, and the police feel that Brandon was already dead. They think that the murder took place at some location, the murderer got in the drivers seat and took off to dump the car where they found it after wiping the wheel.

I took a second to absorb all of that. I knew Brandon had been murdered, but this person was smart. They took the time to make sure they left no fingerprints. They also killed Brandon somewhere else, put his dead body in the car, and drove to the spot and left him there. Why did they kill him though?

"That's not all," the detective added.

My head snapped up.

"The back seat had a large amount of blood. We believe Brandon was leaning into the backseat, or sitting down when the first blows occurred. We found a small pool of blood hidden under some snow in front of the house you all were staying at."

I sat there, confused by what this all meant until it hit me like a ton of bricks. I couldn't breathe. The detective gave me a knowing nod. I thanked him for allowing him insight, and he once again reminded me to call if I figured out anything else. He asked if I wanted to see the evidence, but I passed. I heard enough today. I don't know if I could see anything from the crime in this state.

I went outside and called up the car service. Thankfully, the driver had remained in the area and was only ten minutes away. He arrived, and asked if we were heading back home. I was able to make out a very meek, "Y-yes." He started to drive away, and my exhaustion kicked in.

When I woke up, the driver was telling me we had arrived. I paid him, and quickly excited. I checked my watch. I was in for a nasty argument- I had skipped dinner. I hadn't even closed the front door before I heard my mom's voice. Her angry voice.

"Avery Anne! It is seven thirty at night! I haven't seen you all day. What in God's name were you doing?!"

"Sorry mom. I decided to stay at Macy's all day. We needed some time to talk. I really should have called, I'm sorry."

She gave a sympathetic smile, and pulled a plate out of the oven.

"Well come eat hon, it's still hot."

I hadn't realized how famished I'd been. I had been so busy sleuthing and talking to detectives that I failed to eat something all day."

"They don't feed you over there at Macy's?" she chuckled.

I laughed. "They do, but you know how Macy's mom is all about the "small snacks, not big meals" thing."

I continued to eat my meatloaf and mashed potatoes until I was so full, I couldn't possibly stomach any more. I decided to go upstairs and rinse the worries of the day away with a boiling shower. Like clockwork, I turned the shower as high as it would go, undressed, and stepped under the stream of hot water.

I emerged with less worries, and extremely red skin. My mom always joked about how if I kept it up, one day I would burn all of my skin off. I would always respond saying that it still wouldn't be to my liking.

As I began to get dressed, my phone buzzed with a text message from Jason. My heart soared. Was that pathetic? I hadn't talked to him all day and yearned to hear from him even if it was in a text. The message said:

"Hey Aves, I haven't heard from you all day. Are you okay? How are you feeling? Text back, I miss you, x."

I couldn't help but break into the most Cheshire cat grin. He made me giddy, and I wasn't a giddy person. It was at that moment I remembered what the detective told me, and I felt sick all over again. I texted back:

"Meet up tomorrow morning for coffee? I have news about Brandon. Need to tell someone."

He seemed nervous, but texted back: Okay. I tried to force the thoughts out of my head and get some sleep, but I was overrun with thoughts of Brandon. Nowadays, I always thought of Brandon. Tomorrow, I would be able to talk to someone about it- Jason. I fret over the thought of having to tell him all the information about how Brandon was killed especially the worst part… that he was killed right in front of the house.

# Chapter 7

My alarm went off that morning, and rather than feeling hopeful- I was terrified. I was worried about how Jason would take the news. How could I tell him? Brandon was killed right in front of the house, and then driven six miles away and left like he was garbage. If the Gainespole police department is correct in their findings, then it's more than likely that one of my friends was in fact the killer. That thought itself proved more horrifying than the news of Brandon's murder.

Nevertheless, I knew it had to be done. I needed to start looking at my friends less like the people I grew up with, and more like cold hearted killers. I was reassured by knowing Jason wasn't the killer. We fell asleep and woke up in the same positions, right next to each other on the couch. I had worked out the probability in my head last night, and I don't believe it would have been possible for Jason to remove himself from under me, drag Brandon outside, kill him, drive him away, walk six miles back, wash up, and then lay right back with me without my waking up. I was a heavy sleeper, but not to that level.

I found myself getting dressed extra slow, as if even my body knew of what I was about to face. My phone had started to ring with texts from Jason, and I knew I couldn't put it off any longer. I pulled on my shoes, let my mom know I would be back soon, and headed out the house.

I only lived a few blocks from the coffee shop, so opted to walk. I relished in the cool morning air. Plus, the walk would give me time to decided what I would say. How has this become my life in a matter of days? I couldn't think about that right now and shoved the thought to the back of my mind in true Avery fashion. I couldn't allow myself to wallow, Brandon's murder needed to be solved. I would deal with everything then.

I rounded a corner, and the coffee shop came into view. That oh so familiar pit in my stomach resurfaced as I opened the door and stepped in. I spotted Jason easily dressed in the sweater I got him last year at a table against the wall. He stood out like a sore thumb- in a good way. He had already got our coffees. Naturally, mine was the largest. I was a coffee fiend, what can I say?

"Hey Jason. Thanks for the coffee, I feel like I need it today," I said with a laugh.

"Of course, but I must admit you had me worried. What did you have to tell me about Brandon?"

I guess this was it. This was the moment where I would permanently change Jason's view of our friends. I took a deep breath.

"Yesterday, I went to investigate the house. While I was there, I ran into Detective Greene. Long story short, he gave me some information about Brandon and how he was murdered."

"What?! First off Avery, why would you go there yourself? You know I would have gone with you if you asked."

"I did ask, and you and everyone else practically shut me down. I can't just move on and act like Brandon didn't exist. He deserves justice. Anyhow, I think we have to start looking at ourselves to find the killer."

"What is that supposed to mean," he asked defensively.

"The detective told me that the steering wheel was wiped clean. That means Brandon was not the only one to drive the car, if he drove it at all. They found blood frozen under fresh snow when they investigated the front of the house. They truly believe that Brandon was killed in the backseat and then driven to the place they found the car."

He looked crushed. I wish more than anything I could take this pain away from him, take it unto myself. We loved Brandon. To not only have to cope with his sudden murder, but to come to the realization that it may in fact have been one of our closest friends is more than anyone should have to deal with in their lifetime. We were dealing with it in a matter of seventy-two hours.

All I could do was hug my friend… or whatever we were these days. He embraced me tightly, and then suddenly pulled back. He spoke.

"So… Brandon was murdered by one of our friends?"

I just looked at him and slowly nodded. God, I still couldn't wrap my head around this. The worst part was that all of us hadn't really been in contact since it happened, and I didn't know what was going through their heads.

"I have to visit them."

"No way, I know they're our friends, but at this point we don't know what any of them are capable of."

I finally talked him into the idea of at least letting me visit Macy. She was my best friend, and I know she could barely kill a fly without crying afterwards. Plus, she was going through the same emotions and pain we were, without any support from us. I felt like a bad friend. I have been so focused on solving Brandon's murder, that I neglected my friends in the process. I would see her this afternoon.

I sent a quick text to my friend: Can I stop by today? I miss you, Mace.

Her response was quick: Of course. I have been an absolute mess. Come over whenever.

I hugged Jason and told him I would text him later. He planted a soft kiss on my cheek and reminded me to, "Be careful." I nodded, letting him know I would and headed out. The great part about living in a small town was that you were pretty much walking distance to everything. Macy only lived around the corner from the coffee shop, so I started towards her house still sipping on my liquid fuel.

I must have been nervous, as I found myself counting the steps I took. I was at three hundred and twenty-four when her familiar colonial came into view. Her mom was sitting on the porch sipping out of her mug and reading. That was where you would always find Macy's mom- it was her happy place. If you met her mom, then it made a lot more sense why Macy was the way she was. Macy was truly a reflection of the wonderful woman who raised her.

As I walked up the driveway, her mom spotted me.

"Avery dear! How are you? I've missed seeing you here," and embraced me in a hug.

I squeezed her back. She made me feel comforted. I told her I was doing as well as can be expected, and that I came to see Macy for some girl time.

"Good, because Macy needs it. She's been moping around since she got back. I really wish you children weren't exposed to that level of horror," she said as she shook her head.

I thanked her and headed inside. I wish we weren't exposed to that horror either. It was my job to find out who caused it. I knew Macy wasn't capable of this type of carnage, but Jason wouldn't feel comfortable until she was ruled out. How would I do that?

I bounded up the stairs and found Macy sitting on her bed watching Dateline. Odd choice, considering we were living in an episode now.

"Hey Mace. I missed you. How are you?"

"I feel sad, like all the time. I can't stop thinking about him Avery. He didn't deserve it. What the hell happened," she moaned and put her head in her hands and began to sob.

My tears welled up instantly and I ran over and grabbed my best friend. This was hard for all of us, and I couldn't forget that. Neither of us said anything, but hugged one another, cried, and found comfort in the other. By the time we let go, our eyes were red and puffy. In that moment, I remembered what Lisa had told me- that Macy was there at the scene by herself and that she was frantically looking around the front of it. I decided if I wanted to satisfy Jason, I would confront her about it and clear her name of all suspicion.

"Macy, I hate to bring this up, but I went to the house. I went yesterday to hopefully find some clues about Brandon and what happened."

She looked completely taken aback. "What? Why? Did you find anything."

"Unfortunately, no but I did run into Lisa."

She eyed me cautiously and asked, "What did she say?"

"Well, she said we were not welcome back... and to tell that to my friend who came by earlier the night before."

She was quiet. I was going to ask her what she had been doing there before she finally spoke. "It was after we were talking at the park. I shut you down, because I was scared to find out about Brandon. His death terrifies me. I wanted to go check it out, and see if I could find anything," she said with a sad look before adding, "but I didn't."

"Why couldn't you just say that to me? I thought we could talk about anything."

"I know we can. I just haven't felt like myself. I cry all the time. I thought maybe if I isolated myself from you and everyone else, that I wouldn't be able to bring you down."

"Mace, you could never bring me down. We're all in the same boat. Brandon's death has been so hard on all of us. Please, don't isolate yourself- talk to me."

"I will. I'm sorry I lied to you Avery," she apologized.

"I don't care that you lied, I just don't want you to keep anything from me," and smiled at my best friend.

With that difficult conversation out of the way, maybe my friends and I could begin to heal. I was comforted knowing that Macy wasn't capable of something like this and knew in my heart that she couldn't have killed Brandon. His death destroyed her. That only left two suspects- Joey and Erica.

Those seemed like unlikely killers as well. Erica can't stand the sight of blood, so I seriously doubt she would have been able to stomach killing someone. It would have taken a lot of strength to murder someone of Brandon's size without finding yourself with wounds after. I remembered that with how much Brandon drank that night, a mouse could have overpowered him.

Joey. My kindest, and oldest friend. I couldn't imagine him being able to take someone's life either and especially not Brandon. However, if the facts were true then it had to be one of my friends. I needed to talk to Joey and see what he knew. I had to see if he could have killed Brandon.

# Chapter 8

I said my goodbyes to Macy and her mother, and had Macy promise to not isolate herself. I didn't want my friend to grieve alone. We were all in this together. I hadn't heard from Joey since we all left the police station. It seemed like we all attempted to close ourselves off from one another.

Joey lived next door to me, so not seeing or talking to him was extremely out of the ordinary. We saw each other everyday for the past ten years. Our mothers were best friends, and I had no doubt that they had been in contact the past couple of days no doubt talking about us, and what we were going through.

That was the thing. I knew how desperately all of our parents wanted to fix the situation, fix us. They couldn't. Brandon was dead. He was our best friend, and his absence would leave a lasting mark on each one of us for the rest of our lives. I didn't know how to go through all of the motions, and deal with his death properly. Besides the overwhelming out of tears these last few days, I still hadn't truly faced what had happened. I decided to throw myself into solving this as a means of distraction and to get justice for Brandon. Not only did I want to expose the killer for Brandon's sake, but his mother's.

I can't imagine the pain and trauma she has been through since the news of Brandon's murder broke. She lost her husband years ago in a car crash caused by a drunk driver. Now, to lose her only son just years later must be devastating. The way she looked at me in the police station that day, has been on constant replay in my mind.

I knew the memorial service too. Brandon's mom hadn't been in contact with any of us recently, but my mom heard through the grapevine that due to the amount of damage she opted to have Brandon cremated and his ashes scattered at his favorite beach.

That was Brandon, the fun loving, obnoxiously loud life of the party. The beach remained one of his favorite places to spend time all of these years. He enjoyed surfing and especially beach volleyball.

I debated on going to the memorial. I knew that Brandon's mom was distrusting of not only myself, but my friends too. But, I don't know if I could ever forgive myself if I didn't make the conscious effort to at least be there for Brandon's final send off.

I decided that I would reach out to his mom prior to the memorial and see if she would allow us a chance to talk.

I strolled up the steps to Joey's house and felt a knot in my stomach. How could I look at him the same, when I thought he may have murdered Brandon? I tried to not let that assumption cloud my judgement and give him the benefit of the doubt. He was still my friend after all, and who knows? Maybe it wasn't Joey either. What if the detective was wrong? After all, there could have been someone else. For all we know, Brandon was getting something out of the car when someone killed him. I knew that didn't make sense. There was no reason to kill him. My head felt like it was going to explode. I raised my hand to knock on the door, but nearly fell forward because Joey opened the door at that exact moment.

"Joey! I was going to knock," I explained.

He laughed, "Yeah, I figured it was either that or you're looking for a fight?" He glanced at my still closed fist.

"Right, well can I come in? I wanted to talk," I said as I unclenched my fist.

He stepped to the side and motioned for me to come in. The house was empty like it usually was, but this was the only time that ever made me uneasy. What happened to giving my friend the doubt?

Joey interrupted my thoughts as he embraced me in a hug that lasted several seconds. When he pulled away, he studied my face no doubt looking for clues if I was okay. I forced a smile and asked him how he was doing.

"Not well. I haven't really talked to any of you since the park, besides Erica anyways. If you were wondering, she hasn't been sleeping well either."

"I figured as much. I'm sorry I haven't been over here I just..."

Joey cut me off.

"You've just been... sneaking around? C'mon Avery, we're neighbors. I saw you sneak out of the house the other day. You made a lot of noise slamming that car door."

I hadn't realized that Joey had been paying that much attention to me and my whereabouts. Maybe he was starting to become suspicious of what I knew. Which was nothing. In the past few days, I have done more snooping and investigating than ever before. However, I had nothing to show for it. All I knew was that one of my friends killed Brandon. As I talked to each of them, I hoped for some clarity as to who could have done something this malicious. Rather than finding answers, I feel more confused than ever.

Brandon's death has completely turned my life around. If I had thought a stranger had done it, some lowlife, it still would have hurt but I would have been able to accept what is. The thought that maybe these people who I spent all my time with, told everything to, were the opposite of who I thought they were was absolutely terrifying. I couldn't stomach the thought. I continuously pushed it to the back of my mind, and when I found it resurfacing, I would find another friend to attempt to put the blame on.

"Avery?"

"Sorry, that happens a lot now. Yeah, I did sneak out. I was looking for clues about Brandon's death, so I went back to the house."

I expected Joey to be shocked, and maybe even a little angry. Instead, he was understanding.

"Well, did you find anything?"

"Unfortunately, not. I guess Brandon was killed in front of the house, and then the killer drove the car with him inside and left it at the discovery spot."

Joey looked taken aback, and then completely nauseous. He grabbed the edge of his sofa to steady himself, and then sat down. I understood what he was going through. Hearing that and coming to terms with the truth was a hard pill to swallow. I probably shouldn't have told him about that part. I wouldn't want to tell the killer how much the police knew about what had happened, and then scare him or her off. While my brain was still fuzzy, I knew in my heart that Joey couldn't have done it. Jason, Macy, and Erica couldn't have done it either.

So, who was the killer?

I sat there with Jason for a few hours as we talked about Brandon's death. He didn't bring up the subject of who killed him again. He acted as if I hadn't broken the news that one of our friends was the killer. Maybe he knew more than he was letting on, or maybe he was trying to work it out himself. Either way, I didn't feel that I would be able to get any information out of him. He seemed as lost as I was.

We drank some tea, and when his dad finally arrived home from work, I decided to excuse myself and said my goodbyes.

Once outside, I stood still. I felt like I had hit a wall. There was no new information. The problem was that I simply didn't remember anything from that night, and I desperately needed to. I remembered Erica telling me about a therapist she went to after she lost her mom, who used hypnosis as a way to help.

That was perfect. I would see her, and then hopefully the therapist would be successful in resurfacing forgotten memories from that night.

I called Erica and used my now almost scripted line apologizing about not talking that much recently, said I was dealing with a lot, asked her how she was doing, and then casually asked for the therapist's number. If it were any other time, Erica would have pressed me mercilessly about why I needed the number, but she seemed as if she understood completely why I would seek therapy at a time like this. That seemed to be a gracious effect of this whole thing, people were glad to give you complete privacy.

I called the number Erica gave me and made an appointment with the receptionist who answered the phone for early tomorrow morning. I finally started to feel hopeful. Maybe I remembered more about that night than I thought. Maybe, the therapist can help me to withdraw those memories.

I laid in bed, too exhausted to shower. I was always completely drained at the end of these last few days. I don't know if it was physically or mentally or both. I drifted off to sleep, with the image of Brandon laughing and smiling fresh on my mind.

-----------------------------------------------------------------------

I woke up the next morning to my mom gently shaking me awake. She handed me a cup of steaming coffee in my favorite to go mug and let me know that my alarm had been ringing for the past few minutes.

I turned over and saw that she was right. I switched it off, thanked her, and got out of bed to get dressed. I didn't hear her leave, and my instincts proved true when I turned around and saw her standing in my doorway.

"You doing okay hon? I haven't seen much of you lately."

"I know mom, and I'm sorry. I have been trying to be there for all my friends right now. It's really hard."

"I know it's hard. I couldn't even begin to imagine what you and your friends are going through. I love that you want to be there for them but be sure to also make time to be there for yourself at the end of the day."

She kissed my forehead and walked out of the room. If only she knew.

I pulled on my favorite navy sweater, the coveted leggings, and some converse. I grabbed my phone, keys, and my mug of liquid fuel. The office was a little bit farther than I cared to walk this morning, so I decided to call Jason for a ride.

He was there in fifteen minutes looking absolutely gorgeous. I must admit, seeing him took a little bit of my nerves away. I filled him in on what was happening, and to my surprise he agreed that it would be a good idea for me to go.

We arrived, and Jason agreed to stay in the waiting room while I went in. I signed in and headed through the large red door when she called my name.

I don't know what I expected this therapist to look like, but it certainly wasn't like a supermodel. She had long black hair which seemed to curl around her back, and big brown eyes.

She introduced herself.

"Hi Avery, I'm Dr. Noreen. Take a seat."

She gestured towards a long, beige couch and I sat. We went over the reasons I was here, and she felt that hypnotherapy may be a good shot at recovering any hidden memories from that night. I lied back, and she stood over me.

"Okay Avery, are you ready?"

# Chapter 9

I took a deep breath. I was as ready as I would ever be. I nodded, and she began to talk in a soothing voice.

"Okay Avery, I want you to go to your happy place. Place yourself wherever that may be and take a look around. Soak up your surroundings."

That was easy. My happy place was in a library, surrounded by various books, and clothed in the most peaceful tranquility and comfortable silence. I picture myself sitting in a comfy armchair, with a cup of coffee, and the feel of a great book in my hands.

"Now, I want you to imagine that weekend, and how happy you felt going into it."

Immediately I felt myself tense up. My mind went to Brandon, and my heart seized with the familiar sense of panic I felt that day he went missing, and every day thereafter.

She felt me go rigid and softly reminded me to avert my focus to the happy moments- to push the negative ones to the back of my mind. Oh, I was an expert on that. Instead of focusing on Brandon, I decided to focus on Jason. That helped to recenter my energy and attention on happy feelings. We rekindled us this weekend, and after seven long months were finally able to move past the rut we had been in. Things were no longer weird and awkward with Macy either. Joey and Erica had finally realized what everyone else knew all along- they had feelings for each other.

She continued, "Now I want you to place yourself back in that night. After everyone went to bed, what happened?"

I felt light as feathers and my mind felt at ease. I felt like I was having a dream. I felt Jason's body next to me, and the couch under my back. I could slightly hear hushed voices, and Brandon's voice telling the person to, "Hold on, let me get them." I heard the slight jingle of his keys.

I opened my eyes and felt myself in a cold sweat. I didn't remember that the morning after. The therapist looked pleased with herself, as if she knew she succeeded. I thanked her and rushed out of the office before I was forced to answer any questions.

As promised, Jason was sitting in the waiting room for me. "Let's go," I said abruptly before exiting the bright blue waiting room.

I all but sprinted to Jason's car and reached for the handle, before he caught up to me and grabbed my hand.

"Avery, what happened? You almost tackled me trying to get out of there. Did she do something?"

"Yeah, she did something. She brought back some memories I didn't know I had. I know that's what I came her for, but it wasn't what I was expecting," I said practically out of breath.

"What did you remember?"

I filled Jason in on everything that was brought up. I remembered feeling Jason's body next to me, and the feel of the knit couch under my back. I couldn't see anything, as if I was sleeping when everything happened. I told Jason how I remembered hearing hushed voices before I heard Brandon grabbing his keys. That was it.

"Could you hear the other voice?"

"No, but that's no surprise. Brandon was always the loudest in the room," and I found myself truly laughing for the first time in days.

We both had a good laugh over Brandon's loud voice, that I'm sure we would both give anything to hear right about now. We climbed into the car, and decided to get something to eat since we were both starving. Apparently, the appointment had taken over two hours, but it only felt like minutes. It blew my mind how the hypnotic state worked.

We pulled into one of our favorite mom and pop diners- Hal's.

There were a lot of people who did not care for the run down, old school diners like this one. For me, the ambience of this place was perfect. I much rather eat a home cooked dinner at a place where the people who worked there felt like family. I liked the fact that Al from across the street could always be found at the counter drinking his what seemed like twentieth cup of coffee.

We took a seat in our favorite booth, right across from the jukebox. Almost immediately, our favorite waitress Abby greeted us. She had probably been there the longest and knew the menu like the back of her hand. Her hair was always fastened in these ringlet curls, that framed her heart shaped face. She was a sweetheart.

"Let me guess, two coffees- one with half and half and the other black as night. Am I correct?" she said with a smirk.

"Yes, ma'am," we both chimed in unison.

She turned and glided over behind the counter. Jason stood up and jogged over to the jukebox, quarter in hand.

Before I could see what he was doing, I began to hear my favorite song- "Brave" by Sara Bareilles playing throughout the restaurant.

I couldn't help but smile. Jason was always doing little things to make me laugh, and he knew this song helped me through some dark times. He sauntered back over to the table, complete with a big grin on his face.

"You're sweet, you know that?"

"I know. I also know just how much you have taken on yourself these past few days, and I want you to know that it doesn't have to be that way. I want to help, in any way that I can. I'm only ever a phone call away."

It was right then that I unleashed every emotion I had tried so desperately to suppress these past few days came rushing out in tears. Once I started, I couldn't stop. I missed Brandon so much and trying to keep myself busy with investigating wasn't helping me at all. It was only delaying the inevitable. I needed to say goodbye to my friend one last time. I collected myself just as Abby set down our coffees.

"What can I get you guys to eat tonight?"

"I'll have a turkey burger and fries please," I said excitedly. I loved their burgers.

"I'll have the ham and cheese omelet with hash browns Abby, thanks."

She smiled and headed off to place our order. I breathed a loud sigh. These days seemed to continue to take more and more out of me mentally and after today, physically. I looked at Jason and took a sip of my coffee.

"I want to go to his memorial Jason."

"I heard about that. I can't believe we weren't invited. Brandon was a friend to all of us."

"I know, and that's why I feel as if we should go. I could never forgive myself if I didn't say a proper goodbye. My last memory of him is us helping him into bed."

He stayed silent but gave a look as if he knew. I pulled out my phone and decided to text Brandon's mom. I sent: Hey Mrs. Fuller, it's Avery. I heard about Brandon's memorial tomorrow. I would really love to be there to say my last goodbyes. Would that be alright with you? I hit send.

My phone buzzed a few minutes later with a reply from Mrs. Fuller. It read: Of course, dear. I am so sorry for the way I treated you at the police station. Can I call you later to explain?

I breathed a sigh of relief. The thought of having his mother think I was a killer broke my heart. I wasn't angry with her when she had the outburst at the police station that day. I could not imagine the pain she went through losing her son, and it must have hurt worse not having any answers. I texted back: Sounds good.

I let Jason know that she was okay with our presence but had no time to dwell because just then our steaming hot food arrived. My mouth started watering.

--------------------------------------------------------------------------------

"That was probably the best meal I have ever had."

"While I can admit it was delicious, it probably added to the fact that you had not eaten all day prior," Jason said with a laugh.

I smirked at him as we got into his car. It was easy to fall back into old routines with Jason. I was okay with that though, more than I thought I would ever be after Macy and him. However, I had realized something since Brandon's death, that life is short. I don't want to hold onto resentment, or the past. It weighs heavy on me. I would rather be as open and forgiving as I could. It's how Brandon lived his life- with no regrets.

We drove into my driveway, and I was pulled out of my thoughts.

"Avery, we're here."

"Sorry. Thanks so much for today, Jason. I really needed it. I think it helped me."

"Of course, you know I am always here when you need me."

He gave me a chaste kiss that left my skin feeling like it was on fire.

"Text you?"

"You better," he said and winked.

I got out of the car and turned the lock just as my phone began to ring.

"Miss me already Jason?"

"Oh, I'm sorry dear. It's Brandon's mom."

"No, I'm sorry! I forgot you were going to call. Is it okay to ask how you are doing?"

"It is. I am just taking it day by day. I miss him all the time, he brought such a light into the lives of everyone he met, but you already knew that."

"I did, Brandon was one of the greatest people I have ever known. I am so sorry."

"The reason I was calling was to properly apologize for the incident at the station. I shouldn't have come at you the way I did. It was a rather trying day for me."

"Oh god, I can only imagine. Don't worry about it. I am just glad you don't think I killed Brandon- I could never."

"I know that now dear. You don't have it in you, but I know who does. That bitch Erica killed my son."

# **Chapter 10**

"Erica did what?!"

"She killed my son. I saw for myself how angry she was when he turned her down last month. I have never seen someone so enraged. There's no doubt in my mind."

"I think you're making a mistake… Erica isn't capable of murder."

"If you had seen her that day, you would understand. Listen dear, you and the group are welcome at the memorial. However, Erica is not."

She hung up the phone. I couldn't believe what I was hearing. Mrs. Fuller was absolutely dead set on the theory that Erica killed Brandon. I knew Erica. She freaked out when there was snow in her hair, I do not seriously think that she is able of bashing someone's brains in- especially Brandon. They were close. We all were.

I didn't want to unload this all on Jason, so decided to turn to Macy. I felt a disconnect from my best friend lately, and I knew she would understand just how outrageous this all was.

"Hey Aves, what's going on?"

"Macy, I just got off the phone with Brandon's mom. She apologized for the police station incident, and said we were all invited to the memorial tomorrow."

"That's great news! I would have been devastated if we didn't get to say our good-byes."

"There's one person who will be devastated tomorrow when she finds out she is banned from coming."

"Erica? Who banned her from coming? That is ridiculous."

"Mrs. Fuller. She said that Erica killed Brandon."

"Killed Brandon?! Is this a joke? Erica couldn't hurt a fly. Why does she think that?"

"Apparently, Erica pursued Brandon, but he turned her down-multiple times. Mrs. Fuller said that Erica was furious, and that she had never seen someone so upset."

"Jesus Christ. That does not sound like Erica. She never showed any interest in Brandon! She also doesn't have a temper. This does not make sense."

"I know, but she did not seem like she would change her mind. Maybe we can find some clues tomorrow by asking Erica about it?"

"How are we going to do that if she is not invited," Macy wondered.

"After. We will text her and ask to meet for coffee."

"Sounds like a plan. Text me in the morning."

I said goodnight to my friend, and composed a group text to Macy, Jason, and Joey: Mrs. Fuller said that we are allowed to come tomorrow. She has an issue with Erica coming though, will explain later.

Joey: What exactly is her issue with Erica? If Erica isn't invited, I am not coming either.

Jason: Yeah, what is her deal?

Macy: Okay Aves, see you tomorrow. Love you guys.

I was about to respond, and then send a personal message to Erica until I heard a light pitter patter on my window. I looked outside, and saw Joey tossing pebbles at my windowpane.

I opened the window slightly.

"What the hell are you doing? You know I have a doorbell, right?"

"I didn't want to wake your mom. Come talk to me."

I pulled on a sweater and my slippers, and very carefully tiptoed down the stairs. I was twenty-two and definitely old enough to go out at 11 p.m. but apparently my mother did not get that memo. My mom, unlike myself, was a light sleeper and I did not care to explain this situation to her right now. I was on the last step, and forgetting that it creaked occasionally, found myself wincing when it lived up to its name.

I stopped for a moment to listen for my mother and continued outside when I didn't hear anything.

"Geez Avery, your house is small. It took you ten minutes," Joey scolded.

"I'm sorry! You know how my mom is, so I had to take the stairs one toe at a time," I teased.

My friend didn't look like his happy go lucky self. That was understandable, given that we had just lost our friend, but this was different.

"Are you okay? Something is bugging you; I can tell."

"It's what you said about Brandon's mom not wanting Erica there. Why is that?"

I took a breath. "I guess according to her, Erica came on to Brandon a month ago multiple times, and he turned her down every time. She became livid and was acting absolutely crazy. Brandon's mom is convinced that Erica killed Brandon."

Joey was silent. He opened his mouth to speak, but swiftly closed it as if he was searching for the right words.

"How could anybody ever think that sweet Erica was capable of such violence?"

"I don't know Joey. It has had me thinking about something Jason said one of the nights we were at the house. He said he saw Erica and Brandon arguing."

"And? It was probably alcohol fueled. I doubt either of them remembered anything."

"That is what I said at the time as well, but it has made me think…"

"Think about what Avery? You seriously think Erica could do something like this? That she is capable of murder? Brandon's mom, while extremely off, gets a pass because she's grieving. But you? Looking at her like a suspect? What happened to the Avery who thought the world of her friends? You disgust me."

Joey turned around and stalked off. I felt crushed. I know how close they had become recently, and that she was our friend but as much I hated to admit it- one of our friends killed Brandon. No other theory worked. Maybe it was Erica. I understand Joey's irate behavior considering he has been in love with her for years, but to say I disgust him? That was low. I couldn't even find it in myself to be hurt, because I was furious.

I walked into my house, and without thought, slammed the door. I was so sick and tired of digging myself into holes and finding no answers. I wanted to defend my friends as much as I could, but how much became too much? When was I supposed to step back and accept the truth? And how could I do that when I didn't even know what the truth was yet? I began to sob.

"Avery? What on Earth is going on?"

My mom walked down the stairs in her satin robe and flicked on the lights. She reached for me and held me in her arms. We sat on the couch, and she ran her fingers through my hair and allowed me to cry until I was out of tears. She did not push or ask questions. It was if she knew I needed a moment of silence, and the comfort of my mom to get out all of my emotions. To go from losing a friend in the worst way, to losing another a few days later because he couldn't stand the person, he felt I was becoming was too much to handle.

"I don't want to pry my love, but what happened?"

"It's Joey. I told him that I think Erica killed Brandon, and he told me that the old Avery would have never made an accusation like that. Mom, he said I disgust him," I said as I sobbed into her shoulder once more.

"Oh Avery, why would you say that? I know that the detective said it was one of you but maybe they have their facts wrong. Let me give you a piece of advice- leave the investigating and finger pointing to the police. It's their job. If you do it, you will start to lose friendships my dear. Believe it or not, people don't like to be accused of murder."

I knew she was right. It didn't matter. I knew what she said about the detectives having it wrong, but knowing my mom that bit was added solely for my comfort. I knew that I had to get more information, before I said anything to Joey or Erica for that matter. Those two seemed like a packaged deal, and I didn't want to destroy our friendship more than I probably had tonight.

"Mom, I am going to head up to bed if that's okay. I'm exhausted."

"Of course, love. Just remember what I said," and planted a kiss on my forehead.

　　I ran upstairs to my room and closed the door. I had been unsure earlier, but Joey's reaction and the way he treated me- made me want to be right about this. I hated anything that would hurt Joey, but I had to talk to Erica in person about this. If I was wrong, I didn't want to spread more rumors then I felt I already had. I sent her a text: Hey Erica, can we talk?

Erica: Sure. Meet tomorrow before memorial. Heard I wasn't invited...

I wrote back: I'm sorry. Brandon's mom was adamant. I tried but she was dead set.

Erica: That makes sense I guess considering what happened. Explain tomorrow? Coffee shop, 8 a.m.

　　I responded back letting her know that was okay. I couldn't stop thinking about what Erica had said, "considering what happened." I wasn't sure if she was referring to the passes she made at Brandon, and how he rejected her or if she was about to confess to me. I was so nervous and didn't know how to process so I called Jason. He was the one person who I hadn't explained Mrs. Fuller's ban to, so I felt I should elaborate.

"Hey Avery, I'm glad you called. What was that business with the memorial about? Why wouldn't Erica be invited?"

"I talked to Mrs. Fuller. She said that a while ago, Erica made some passes at Brandon and that Brandon rejected her. Mrs. Fuller said Erica was furious. She is adamant that Erica was the one who killed Brandon."

"Erica? I wouldn't exactly put Erica and killer in the same sentence Aves. You know she could never do that, don't you?"

"Normally yes. I did remember how at the house you mentioned that you had seen those two arguing. What if she made an advance again that night, and when he rejected her, she turned violent?"

"C'mon Avery. She was right across from us. I think we would have heard if she got up, got him outside, and killed him. Even if we didn't notice, Joey would have. He's a light sleeper Avery."

I felt horrible. I felt as if I was ruining Erica's character by being very public about my concerns. The only person I should be talking to was Erica, to give her a chance to explain. Everything my friends were saying was true. Erica wasn't capable of murder. The issue was that none of my friends were. Figuring this out would be the death of me.

"Avery? You still there?"

"Talk tomorrow Jason. Bye." I hung up the call.

Maybe I was right that day to do the investigating alone. Dragging my friends along and into my theories seemed to only be causing more troubles, more confusion, and more fights. They were all right about me though. I was someone who thought the world of my friends. That was exactly why I needed to get justice for one of the best people I had ever known in my life.

Brandon was so kindhearted and never said a bad word about anyone, especially his friends. He had the most amazing moral views and was very adamant about doing the right thing- always. Brandon was an amazing person. He died in a way that no one should ever have to go out especially that young, and at the hand of someone you trusted.

That took a level of hatred and violence that I didn't feel that any of my friends could do, in my heart. However, I decided that to solve this, I would need to start using my head and stop thinking about these people like the kids I grew up with.

They were suspects. All of them. Erica was just at the top of my list now.

# **Chapter 11**

I woke up that morning to my alarm chirping away. I can't remember the last time I was able to go to bed without making sure an alarm was set. Unfortunately, these days, my life seemed to be a set schedule.

I dreaded the conversation I was about to have with Erica. I knew that I needed the truth, whatever the truth may be. If Erica didn't do it, then I was glad. I didn't want any of my friends to be killers, but that was the truth I had been forced to deal with. Macy, Jason, Joey, Erica… all my friends. All suspects. Remember that, Avery.

After my small bout of pumping myself full of confidence, I felt ready to face Erica. She was my friend for years, why did I suddenly feel like I was having coffee with a stranger? I decided to opt for the comfy clothes, as I felt I would be uncomfortable regardless. I pulled my hair into a messy bun, pulled on my favorite boots, and began to walk.

As always, the walk cleared my mind. I loved the way the air was able to allow you to slow time down in your brain, and mentally dissect all the tidbits that were causing you to feel stressed. I always felt better after a walk, and today was no day to skip that.

I rounded the corner and spotted the town coffee shop. I was so nervous, and my palms began to sweat. I was never a confrontational person, as much as I tried to be. I puffed out my chest a little and went inside. Sure enough, I spotted Erica at the counter waiting for me. Naturally, she was decked out in tight jeans, and flowy top decked out in red flowers, and sky-high heels. She looked ready for the runway. Meanwhile, I looked like I hadn't seen a shower in days.

She peeled her eyes away from her phone long enough to spot me. Her face lit up.

"Avery! God, I haven't seen you in days. I missed you, how are you?"

"I'm good, just been trying to deal with each day as it comes. You? I'm sorry we haven't seen much of each other; it's been really hard."

"Don't worry about it. Plus, Joey has really stepped up and been there for me when I needed him. We've kind of been leaning on each other a bit. It doesn't make it easier, but it makes it less hard. I don't know if that makes sense," she smiled.

My sweet friend. She seemed as if she was healing the right way. Instead of running herself ragged like I was, she found comfort in Joey and apparently, he found the same in her. It warmed my heart, seeing them so happy. My heart felt crushed for what I was about to do.

"Sorry to cut to the chase, but I talked to Brandon's mom, Erica."

"I know. I heard about her banning me from attending Brandon's memorial. It sucks, it really does. It is her son though, and I won't ruin the day by showing up if she does not want me there."

"The reason she doesn't want you there is because she thinks you killed her son."

Erica went silent. Her eyes grew large, and she pulled me over to the corner of the coffee shop and into the seats of a small table.

"She thinks I KILLED Brandon? Is she nuts? Why would I ever do something that heinous?"

"Apparently, it's because you acted pretty livid when Brandon turned you down."

She gave a cold laugh. "She told you about that, huh?"

"I didn't hear the whole story, but essentially she gave me the CliffsNotes version."

"Get comfortable Avery, because it's a long story."

"About a year ago, do you remember that party at the Evans house? Well, Brandon and I both got really drunk that night. To the point where we were about to pass out. Well, we both found a room to sleep in. Later that night, I got up to get a drink of water and funnily enough found Brandon in the kitchen doing the same thing. He had sobered up a bit, as had I. I don't know what it was, but we started to kiss, and that led to other things. It wasn't until five weeks later that I found out I was pregnant. I told him, and to my surprise he was overjoyed. That was the kind of guy he was, always supportive. We decided to give us a go, for the sake of our baby. Three weeks after that, we decided it was time to tell you guys about us- and about our child. The night before we were going to reveal it, I had the worst stomach pains of my life. Brandon rushed me to the E.R. but it was too late. I had lost the baby…" and she continued.

"That was the worst night of our lives. We were unsure if we wanted to remain together now that there was nothing truly tying us together. We gave it the benefit of the doubt but started to fall apart shortly after because we were devastated over the loss of our baby. One day at his house, Brandon decided that it wasn't working and broke it off with me. I panicked. I lost my baby, and now I was losing him. No one else knew, and I felt so alone. Brandon's mom got home just as we were in the middle of my freak out. So yes Avery, I was livid. I had every right to be. I didn't kill Brandon, I loved him. I still do. But how long can you love someone who doesn't love you the same way?" she asked with tears in her eyes.

"I'm so incredibly sorry… I didn't think…" I couldn't find the words.

"You're right Avery. You didn't think. You just assumed, like always. You actually thought I murdered Brandon? You think that low of me? I would have done anything for him. He was the love of my life, and the father of my child- alive or not. What you did- it's unforgiveable."

She stormed out, and I was left to my own demise. I sure knew how to make a mess of things. If you had told me to take a wild guess on what happened between Erica and Brandon, I would have never in a million years guessed this. My heart ached for my friends, and for the baby that they mourned privately for so long. I can't believe I accused her of murdering Brandon. Maybe Joey was right, I didn't recognize the person I was becoming.

The memorial was in forty minutes. I needed to be there. I needed to say goodbye to Brandon. I called Macy and asked if I could meet her at her house and borrow some clothes.

"Of course, you can. See you soon Aves," and hung up.

I pretty much sprinted the distance to Macy's house, and was there in three minutes flat. She opened the door before I had the chance to knock.

"Jeez Avery, you look like hell," she said with a laugh and added, "Let's fix that." She pulled me inside.

We went up to her room and as she was picking out clothes, I unloaded the entirety of the morning's events onto her. She was shocked, and I could tell her heart went out to both of our friends, Erica and Brandon.

"I cannot believe they went through something like that and did not tell us."

"Me neither and, now I feel even worse as I all but put her on trial for Brandon's murder."

"Don't feel bad Avery, you had no idea. Plus, you are just trying to get justice for Brandon. I get that. Just maybe, ease up on all the accusations. I think that we all want to find his killer but pointing the finger at all of your friends will ultimately hurt their feelings more than anything."

She was right. I wanted to find Brandon's killer more than anything, but at what cost? I didn't want to destroy all my friendships and connections in the process of doing so. I needed to take a step back and examine all the facts before I decided to steamroll more of my friends.

"Here. This will look great on you," she said as she handed me a black dress that was scoop neck and hugged my curves while also being modest.

It was perfect, and even if it's wasn't- it would have to do. The memorial was in twenty minutes, we were fifteen minutes away, and I will be damned if I am going to be late for this.

I sent a group text to all of my friends: Macy and I are leaving now. We will see you guys there.

Jason: Leaving now as well. Meet you by the car.

Not to my surprise, Joey and Erica did not reply. I knew Erica was still freshly pissed off at me, but Joey and I had not gone this long without speaking or being angry with each other although I did feel that the anger was very much one sided in this case.

I didn't want to upset my friends any more than I felt I already had, so I let it go there. I wouldn't let this go though. I would call Joey and Erica tonight and profusely apologize.

Macy and I were about five minutes away when I got a private text from Joey. It read: I talked to Erica, and she told me everything. I can't believe you Avery.

I put my head in my hands. Could this day get any worse? We pulled into the parking lot and I spotted Jason immediately. He was nicely dressed in black dress pants, and a charcoal colored dress shirt complete with a black tie. He was so handsome.

He began to walk over to us, and I glanced over and saw Brandon's mom talking to family. She waved me over and I told Jason and Macy I would be back in a minute. When I reached her, she enveloped me in a tight hug.

"Thank you so much for coming today dear. I know it would mean the world to Brandon, having his friends here."

"About that, I'm sorry but Joey isn't here. I think he's with Erica in fact."

"I figured as much. Joey's mom told me that those two had been close lately. That's fine though, I wouldn't want anyone associated with that little murderer here today disturbing our peace."

"I actually talked to Erica, and I don't think you understand what you saw that day. They actually were a couple and had gone through some pretty traumatizing things together. I won't say what mostly because it just isn't my place," I grabbed her hand and continued, "Just please trust me on this. Erica didn't kill Brandon."

She looked as if she was considering it for a moment and looked contrite. She opened her mouth to speak but was pulled away by a family member.

The ceremony was about to start. I rejoined my friends and we started towards the beach, shoes in hand. The feeling of the sand under our bare toes was exquisite. Brandon's mom picked a perfect place to lay Brandon. He really did love the beach and was always pulling us with him when he went. I missed him.

Brandon's mom began to give a eulogy on what a great person he was, as if we didn't know. She explained that he always made her proud, and even when he made mistakes- he went out of his way to make things right. She asked if anyone else wanted to say a few words, and to my surprise I felt my arm shoot right up.

I walked up there, unsure of what I would say, unsure of if I could handle my emotions. I took one look at the sand and found my inspiration.

"Brandon was one of those people who always lived on the bright side of life. There was never any situation that was unfixable, and he spent most of his days here soaking up the sun, sand, and the attentive glances from the older sunbathers."

I stopped and felt myself beginning to choke up. I looked at the crowd and found Jason and Macy's comforting smiles, and continued,

"He was always smiling, and I think we can all agree that we always *heard* Brandon before we saw him. He always wanted to make sure people were happy and enjoying life. Life will never be the same without him, and I feel so eternally grateful that I was blessed with having him in my life, even for a short time. To know him was to love him. I'll love you forever, Brandon. I miss you every day."

With that, I handed my mic to the family member standing off to the corner of the amplifier. I gave a final look to my friends, when something caught my eye up on the steps leading down to the beach. I saw Joey and Erica, holding hands and both crying. I started towards them, but upon spotting me they began walking away. My heart hurt but found joy in the fact that we were all here, one last time, for our friend Brandon.

The memorial service from then on out was absolutely beautiful. More of Brandon's family members spoke, as well as Macy and Jason both recollecting fond memories that spoke to Brandon's wonderful character.

After the ceremony was over, I made sure to say goodbye to Brandon's mom. Mrs. Fuller had been a nonstop ball of tears the whole time, but for the first time since the murder I think they were actually happy tears. She knew how much her son was loved, but to hear about the wonderful things he did and the impact he made on other people's lives probably helped her in ways I can't imagine.

"I'm sorry, Mrs. Fuller. Brandon's memorial was absolutely beautiful. Thank you for allowing us to come."

"Of course, dear. Brandon would have wanted all of his friends here. I thought about what you said, about Erica. I did rush to judgement. As a parent, you think you know everything that goes on in your child's life, but I see now that maybe that isn't the case. Please give my deepest apologies to Erica, and I sincerely hope I didn't cause any issues between you guys," she said with kindness in her voice.

I gave her a hug one last time, and found Macy and Jason waiting by the cars. We all hugged, and I promised to have Macy's clothes washed and back to her soon. She laughed. Jason pulled me to the side and asked if I was okay. I let him know that I was, and that everything would start to get better.

Just then, my phone rang, and it was a number I didn't recognize. I answered it, and realized it was my neighbor. When he began to tell me the reason behind the call, I gasped and dropped my phone.

I turned to my friends, who now looked concerned. "That was my neighbor. He said there are police all over my house searching for evidence."

We all got into the car and rushed over to my house. We made it there in fifteen due to Macy driving well over the speed limit. When we got there, my eyes surveyed the scene. There had to be at least five cop cars, and I spotted Detective Greene standing in the driveway staring at me, almost like he had been waiting. "Detective Greene, what the hell is going on?"

He handed me a piece of paper. "This is a warrant to search your house for evidence pertaining to the murder of Brandon Fuller. You are our prime suspect."

# **Chapter 12**

I couldn't believe what I was hearing. Me, the prime suspect? How was that possible? I didn't do it. They needed evidence proving that I did something, didn't they? This didn't make any sense. I turned to my friends who both looked terrified. Macy squeezed me, and Jason grabbed my hand.

"What gave you grounds for the warrant?"

"We discovered new evidence from that night. Apparently, some of your friends heard you and Brandon talking and they also heard you go outside with him."

"My friends?" I turned to Macy and Jason who both looked equally confused.

"Avery, I was asleep next to you. I know you didn't go outside with Brandon... that was impossible," Jason said.

"Of course, I never said anything. I know you didn't do it, you would never. These detectives apparently have their facts wrong," she said and scowled at Detective Greene.

"I never said you two were the ones that said it," Detective Greene said smugly.

"Erica and Joey? There's no way they would say that. It isn't true. I was asleep all night, so they would be lying. My friends wouldn't do that to me..."

Just then a police officer came out of the house, holding something in a bag and called Detective Greene over. They spoke for several minutes and Detective Greene returned.

"What is it?"

"Avery Grant, you're under arrest for the murder of Brandon Fuller."

He began to read my rights, and much to my friend's protest, walked over and put me in the squad car. How was this happening? I didn't kill Brandon. What the hell could they have possibly found? None of this made any sense! My mom got home from work at that time, and Macy ran over to her and seemed to give her the news of what was happening. I saw my mom start to cry, and her and Macy hugged. Jason just looked openmouthed at the car, in complete shock.

I mouthed, "I didn't do it," to Jason as a way of reminding him I wasn't capable of something like this. He must have already known, because he mouthed back," I know."

The car started off to the local police station. Apparently, this was now in my city's jurisdiction considering I live here.

We arrived, and there were reporters everywhere. All I could see were flashes, and I heard what seemed like a million people trying to ask me questions at once.

"Avery, why did you kill your friend?" one reporter asked.

"Was it self-defense?"

I couldn't take this. I could never kill someone, let alone my best friend. What could they have found that gave them grounds to arrest me? This was absolute insanity. I have never felt more terrified in my life.

Why would Erica and Joey lie to the detectives? Oh god, what if I was right about her all along? Would they really go as far as to frame me? I could maybe understand Erica, but that didn't seem like something Joey would do. I felt so betrayed, and I didn't have time to dwell on it, because they began taking my picture, and doing my fingerprint.

This was serious. I was really going to jail. Oh god, I couldn't breathe.

"Avery Grant, please step forward."

I was in a long line, and they were moving me into a small cell. I was apparently waiting for my lawyer. I couldn't believe that it has come to this.

They closed the metal door and slid the lock. I sat on the edge of the cool metal seat and cried. I couldn't stop crying, in fact. I was innocent. This wasn't fair. How would I prove to everyone that I was innocent, when the people I thought were my friends had done such a stellar job making me look guilty?

I continued to sob, until I ran out of tears. I pulled myself up straighter. As much as I wanted to curl into a ball and hide, there was no way I would allow myself to let them win. Joey and Erica had to know they weren't going to be able to break me. I had love for my friends, but what they did is unforgivable. I would get out of here, I would find justice for Brandon, and I would sure as hell clear my name.

There was a swift knock on the door, and it opened to reveal a tall blonde-haired man in a nice suit. He introduced himself as Gregory Baine, my lawyer. The fact that I needed an attorney showcases juts how much "deep shit" I had gotten myself in to.

Gregory had the officers escort him and I to a private room where we would be able to discuss details of my arrest and my hearing that was apparently set for the morning.

"This is moving so quick. I don't understand."

"I know, the fact that they are speeding the process along means they think they have an open and shut case. They are pretty positive you'll be convicted."

"But how can I be convicted if I'm not guilty. I didn't do it Gregory you have to believe me. Someone has to believe me!"

"It doesn't matter whether or not I believe you, but you need to somehow convince the jury to believe you. Tomorrow is a hearing where we will discuss housing until the trial starts. I will push for you to stay with your mother until the start of the trial, and I have no doubt the prosecution will push for remand."

"I don't understand why they're so sure I did it. What did they find?"

"Apparently, they found a shirt in your closet. It was covered in Brandon's blood."

"What? That's impossible. I didn't kill him. Even if I had, I wouldn't be stupid enough to leave it lying in the most obvious spot they would look. I have seen enough law and order shows to know better."

"Regardless, they tested it, and it is a sure match to Brandon's blood. The shirt and your friend's testimony make this a slam dunk. They have had trouble finding the murder weapon."

"I can't help you there. I don't even know how he was killed."

"Apparently, the fragments left in Brandon's skull were something similar to a brick or a large rock."

"Jesus. This is all too much for me."

"I know, and I'm sorry. I will be here first thing in the morning to escort you to the hearing. Get some rest," and with that he headed out.

I couldn't process anything right now. I could only think of my family, and my friends. My mom must have been going crazy out of her mind worried about me. I hoped she knew that I didn't do this and would stick by me. I hoped that Jason and Macy were okay. I saw how destroyed they looked when I was put in handcuffs. They were my true friends. Erica and Joey were dead to me. All of the years of friendship seemingly go right out the window when they lie to the police and get me arrested for murder.

So, I had a hearing tomorrow. This was really going to trial, and I could really get put away for a crime I didn't commit. I sat down in my cell and decided to try my best to piece everything together, but that was hard when it made little to no sense.

For one, I know that Joey and Erica lied to the detective. They told him that they heard me talking to Brandon that night, and that we went outside together. It's pretty convenient that all of this came up after I started asking them questions and looking at Erica as a suspect. I dropped that idea after she told me about the baby. I realized that my friend wasn't capable of murder. Apparently, she was capable of framing me. They couldn't have done this out of anger, it was insane. No, they were covering something up. They had to be.

How did the shirt get in my room? Joey. He lived next door and would easily be able to get in and get out undetected. He knew exactly where we hid all the spare keys, and I hadn't exactly been a homebody lately. I was in disbelief. They had the shirt in their possession, and according to my lawyer it tested positive for Brandon's blood. That was the shirt the killer was wearing when he was killed. One of them killed Brandon. Now, I just had to find my way out of this mess they made for me and prove it.

I had to clear my name.

I knew I still had one call. Joey and Erica were pointless to call, they would just hang up or deny everything. It was between Jason, Macy, and my mom. I wanted so badly to call my mom and feel her comfort. She would have to know I didn't do this. Right? A part of me also yearned to hear my best friend, to explain, and to seek her advice. However, I found myself dying to hear Jason's voice tell me it would all be okay. I asked for my one call and dialed the number.

"Jason?"

"Avery! Oh my god. I can't believe you're in jail, this whole thing is insane! Your mom has been crazy dialing every attorney she could find, and she has been speaking with the detective all night but it's useless. He won't give her any information."

"You're at my house? Is Macy there? Where's my mom?"

"Those two are exhausted. They're both passed out on the couch. I've been sitting her trying to make sense of this whole thing. It's a mess."

"Well, that makes two of us."

He sighed, "I'm sorry Avery. I can't think of a worse person for this to happen to. All you have been trying to do since Brandon died was find his killer. I can't believe Joey and Erica would make up some shit like that. To know he's right next door at this very moment too…"

"Jason don't do anything. He's not worth a hair on your head. But, if you did kick the crap out of him then I might be getting myself a cell mate," I chuckled.

"I wouldn't. I mean I would, but you're right. He's not worth it. I will be there at the hearing tomorrow. We all will. Macy has been a wreck all night. She's scared for you, we all are. But don't worry Aves it will all be okay."

I breathed a sigh of relief. "That was just what I needed to hear, thanks Jason. I will see you tomorrow, sleep tight." I hung up.

The policeman walked me back to my cell, and soon enough I heard that familiar bolt lock. I wonder if I could break out of here. Yeah, that probably wouldn't pan out too well for my, "I'm innocent" defense. I laid down on the scratchy cot and attempted to get some sleep. I had to look presentable tomorrow.

I was woken too early, but I had to pull myself together. Today would be the deciding factor if I had to spend the days of my trial locked in this brick box that smelled horrible, or in my home surrounded by the comfort of my family and real friends. I gave myself a little pep talk before heading out. You got this. You have nothing to be afraid of.

I walked into the courtroom, and my stomach felt as if it was doing a thousand somersaults. The judge was a stern-faced older woman, and I could already tell she had a chip on her shoulder. I turned and just as promised, saw my mom, Jason, and Macy all in the first row giving me sympathetic glances, and mouthing "We love you," in unison.

"Order. Can the defendant rise?"

I did as she said.

"Avery Grant, you are being charged with second degree murder. How do you plead?"

"Not guilty, your honor."

"Okay, a trial date will be set for the following week. The defendant will be released into her mother's custody with the requirement she wear an ankle monitor. Any objections?"

The prosecutor spoke up, "Due to the nature of these crimes, and the fact that the defendant was in the possession of an item that took place during the murder, we request remand."

"Save the evidence for the trial prosecutor. But remand, granted. See you next week. Court is adjourned."

I turned to my lawyer slightly panicking, "What does that mean?"

"It means you will be sent to stay in prison until your court date. I'm so sorry."

I got one last look at my mother, and friends before being taken away by the bailiff.

# **<u>Chapter 13</u>**

I felt broken- mentally and physically. I've lost Brandon, my freedom and two of my so-called friends hate me enough to try and get me sentenced for a murder I didn't commit. I remember feeling so bad when I was asking Joey and Erica those tough questions, but now I can see that the problem was that I was asking all the right ones.

Thankfully, the judge didn't take away my visitation rights. My mom visited almost every day, and Jason and Macy came to see me whenever they had a free moment. All three of them were working vigorously to uncover any evidence they could.

My lawyer said that while the words of Joey and Erica wouldn't have been enough to convict me as it is hearsay, the shirt was pretty much the nail in my coffin. The lawyer wanted me to look on the bright side: they had not found the murder weapon. Oh joy.

I'm sure Joey and Erica are plastering my DNA all over whatever weapon was used right now. I can't believe I ever called these people my friends. They were willing to send me to prison, to make me the scapegoat. The crazy part is that even through all of this- my heart ached for Brandon.

How could I feel so down on myself that I was stuck in this prison, while Brandon was gone forever. My lawyer was right in that I needed to start looking on the bright side, but it was hard to see any bright side in a dimly lit ten by ten room with no windows. I had just choked down what they call "breakfast" here. I was grateful that I was in a cell by myself. I don't know if I could face anyone else right now besides Macy, Jason, and my mom. They were the only people I trusted, but I hadn't been such great company lately.

I know my first trial date was only a week away, but my mom was sending me money to be able to buy snacks for myself and sent me books as a means of distraction. I was able to read three books a day if I wanted to, so she wanted me to be stocked up.

That was something I always loved about books, that they could take you out of your reality for a moment and give you the gift of stepping into someone else's world- the ability to leave all your problems behind even if it was for a short time. Regardless of what she sent I couldn't take myself out of this.

I was in deep, and no romance novel set in the 60's would change that. My mom was very careful in her selection of what genres she sent me. When she brought the very first book in, a romantic book about cowboys, she made sure to note that she stayed away from the "murder mystery" section. My mom thought she was hilarious. I laughed at the pitiful joke as a way to make my mom feel better.

I knew she was struggling immensely and using humor as a way to distract from her real feelings and make a joke out of the situation. A part of me was grateful. I don't know if I could continue to let her visit if she just stared at me with that look of pity on her face- the same face Macy had on every visit. I didn't want to be pitied, it only made me feel worse. I wanted to laugh, and to forgot even for just a moment that I wasn't locked in my personal version of hell.

It had been about four days since I was sent to here to stay for the duration of my trial and who knows? Maybe I would get to be a permanent resident. The trial wasn't looking good. The only evidence we had was my word against two other people.

Jason offered to say that we were next to each other all night. But we both knew that not only would Dumb and Dumber dispute that, but the prosecution would argue that someone who is a heavy sleeper would definitely not be able to notice if the person next to them got up. Macy even offered to lie on the stand and say that she heard Brandon talking to Erica, not me, but I wouldn't let her commit perjury on the stand.

I was innocent, and I wouldn't allow my friends to become guilty as a way to get me out of here. It went against everything I stood for. I had been raised to take everything in strides. I refused to stoop to Erica and Joey's level, but my lawyer was adamant about reconciling with them. He had hopes that after that, they would retract their lies or say they forgot.

It absolutely killed me to do this. I couldn't bear to look at them, but I found myself dialing Joey's number. It rang for what felt like forever, and then went to voicemail. I tried Erica, and it was the same thing.     At least I could tell my lawyer I tried.

Normally, I was someone who could easily forgive and forget. However, this crossed the line. I was sitting in jail! If the trial went bad which I had a feeling it would, then I would be sentenced to prison. Everything I worked for my whole life, my schoolwork, and my lifelong dream to be a teacher would vanish just like that. It was no longer about some petty disagreements; this was my life on the line. I would be damned if I didn't fight for the right to live it outside of these walls. I had to.

While I was stuck here, I figured I would at least try to be friendly. Most of these women were in here for crimes they *actually* committed, and I wanted to tread as carefully as possible. I mean Macy and Jason couldn't visit me all day long, so I had to do something.

While most of the interactions I had with the other inmates were small and just your casual greeting, there was one younger woman who seemed to take a liking to me. The first thing she ever said to me was that I didn't look like I belonged here. I jokingly said, "Why? Too tough?"

She thought I was a riot. I don't know why I felt comfortable spilling the entire contents of my life story to her, but I did. I explained the situation I was in, and why I was here.

"So, you're being convicted for the murder of your friend, but it's your other friend that did it? And those friends framed you for it?"

"I know, it's a lot of keep up with."

Her and I bonded over the feeling of constant isolation. While her cell was to the left of mine, she and I were similar in that we were alone in our cells. Some females were kept solely by themselves if they felt a danger to others was prominent.

Yeah, I should've seen that one coming. I guess "killing a man" is enough grounds to label you as "volatile" and "a danger to others".

As much as I hated being here, I vowed to look at every day with the glass half full attitude. I wanted to honor Brandon's memory in the only way I knew possible. He was always so happy and had a genuine positivity about him, always. I vowed to stay positive until the very end of this.

I would be lying if I said I wasn't scared. I was terrified of spending my life paying for something I was innocent of. However, I couldn't worry about that now. Right now, I had to focus on getting out, and getting cleared.

It was T minus two days until the trial date would start. I took some comfort in knowing that the case usually wouldn't be solved in one hearing, and I had another week at least to put off the inevitable- my verdict being decided.

Today, Jason was visiting, and I felt my heart soar. The dark cloud that had been over my head in this hell hole was finally starting to diminish and I could see the beautiful sky and shining sun again.

I was told that Jason was here, and I was led out to the visiting area. He looked gorgeous in a white knit sweater, and his favorite pair of blue jeans. His hair was styled in that messy but still perfect kind of way. I felt inadequate in my orange jumpsuit and raggedy hair. I tried to brush it and smooth it out as much as I could, but this was as good as it was going to get with no flat iron or smoothing serum in sight.

"Hey beautiful, how are you holding up?"

"I have never so much as cheated on a test, and I'm casually sitting in jail hanging out with a bunch of felons. I've never been better!"

He winced. "I'm sorry Aves. I tried to call Joey, and even Erica but neither are answering their calls. I have been staying at your house a lot more recently to keep your mom company. Come to think of it, I haven't seen Joey at all."

"Well, they're probably living together now. You know what they say- those who lie and sent innocent people to jail together, stay together!"

He couldn't help but laugh. "I see you haven't lost that fire in you."

"Never, life would be dull without it. I missed you," and reached for his hand.

His hand found mine, and he gave a gentle squeeze. He smiled at me and leaned in to kiss me before the guard interrupted. They had this little rule about being a certain distance apart.

It only gave me more motivation to keep my spirits high, and the hope alive that I would be out of here soon.

"How's Macy doing? I know she came by a few days ago, but she seemed sad."

"Macy is doing everything she can to find a loophole. She is running herself ragged, and it leaves her a little more worn down than usual."

"I don't want her to kill herself trying to save my ass. That's what the lawyer is for anyways," and I winked. I desperately needed to lighten the mood. Talking about how royally screwed I was made me feel, well, royally screwed.

"How's Rufus?" I asked changing the subject. Rufus was Jason's golden retriever since he was a kid. The dog was old, but still was able to sprint like you wouldn't believe.

"He's good, but he's getting up there. Mom said he's been slowing down recently. Don't change the subject though."

"I just want to talk about anything but the trial Jason, please."

"Okay, you're right. How about we discuss us? What are we Aves?"

"You're asking me now…while I'm locked up?"

"It's the perfect time. Avery, ever since you were arrested and been here- I have felt like a piece of my heart has been living outside my body. I haven't been able to sleep."

"I feel the same way Jason, so what does that make us? Are we a couple? Are you even ready for that?"

"I've been ready," and he gave my hand a squeeze.

"That settles it then, you're my boyfriend," I said with a huge grin.

"And you're my girlfriend," he said as he kissed my hand.

"VISITING IS OVER, LEAVE YOUR BADGES WITH THE DESK."

"Ah, little fun killer that one is. I guess that's my cue. See you tomorrow?"

"I wouldn't miss it," as he winked.

I was led back to my cell, with a new outlook that had my hopes high. I needed to get out. I wanted to be with Jason. I wanted to be able to drink mimosas with Macy at Sunday brunches. I wanted to fall asleep on the couch next to my mom watching Twilight reruns. I wanted to have my freedom back.

I ate my dinner in silence that night, constructing a plan for the hearing. It finally came to me. As long as there was one juror who found me not guilty, they would be deadlocked regardless if the other ninety nine percent thought I was guilty- ultimately causing a mistrial. Right now, it seemed like it would be my only chance of getting out. I didn't need to convince the whole jury of my innocence, just one.

# Chapter 14

I couldn't contain my excitement this morning. Jason was visiting today, and so was Macy. Apparently, my lawyer planned to stop by and "strategize" as well. It was going to be a busy day, but in here, I appreciated the distractions. It was when I slowed down, that my mind began to wander. That was dangerous.

I can't even count the number of times I had "tidied" my cell since I had been here. I don't really know how you can tidy up a cell with maybe four things in it, a toilet, sink, bed, and my personal items. That was it. I constantly rearranged my books and snacks. My mom had brought me a pad and paper when she was here, and it helped to journal out a lot of what I was feeling.

I found writing relaxing. I was always overthinking, and jotting things down almost allowed me to clear out my head a bit. Needless to say, I found myself drawing chart after chart trying to connect the dots in this whole case. They never did find the murder weapon. Maybe if they did, they would see that my fingerprints weren't on it, but I guess that didn't really matter considering they had the shirt.

I had still yet to see this shirt, but my lawyer assured me that everything would come out when the trial started. Considering it was the prosecution's one solid piece of evidence against me, they would be sure to show it.

My mom had gone shopping and called to let me know she would be sending an outfit with Macy today for me to wear the first day of the trial.

To lighten the mood, I asked her to go for more "homeless shelter volunteer" and less "cold blooded murderer", and you can probably guess she didn't find that very funny.

All I ever wanted to do since I found out it was one of my friends killed Brandon, was protect them. In fact, it took me a while to even consider the idea that one of them did it.

I slowly started to cross people off my suspect list, Macy was first. Needless to say, it didn't take much to take her off. Then came Jason, Joey, and Erica. Erica only became a real suspect in my eyes after Brandon's mom accused her of murder.

That's when I think my perspective on my friends changed, only for me to feel bad when I found out the reason behind the issues with Erica and Brandon- their miscarriage. I felt so horrible about it and tried to make amends, but Erica considered what I done to be "unforgiveable" while Joey was "disgusted with me". They even went as far as to plot my demise and lie to detectives. It was their lie that gave Detective Greene the grounds for his warrant. Without the warrant, there would be no discovery of an obviously planted shirt.

The more I thought about it, the more I began to realize how well the timeline was put into place. I didn't see exactly where they found the shirt, but I knew they found it in the closet. If you didn't realize by the fact that I was continuously cleaning my cell, I am a very tidy person. My closet is spotless. The clothes are even organized in color sections. I have a small shelf on top which has all my shoes in organized slots. Where the hell would the bloody shirt have been put where I didn't notice?

When I got dressed that morning, I didn't see anything out of the ordinary in my closet. It must have been planted after I left the house to meet Erica, and who better to do so than Joey. It's all very convenient that the day Detective Greene is able to get a warrant, is the same day that a bloody shirt shows up in my closet haphazardly.

My thoughts were interrupted by the familiar noise of the bolt unlocking and my cell door opening up.
"You have visitors."

Finally. This day was starting to look up.

When I stepped into the room and saw my best friend and boyfriend, I felt so overwhelmed with love and joy. I was so glad to see Macy, and she looked better than the last time I saw her. She looked well rested, and that made me feel a little bit more relaxed, knowing she wasn't killing herself trying to help me out. Jason looked handsome as ever. They were both sporting gifts in their hands. Jason had something in a box and Macy had a familiar gold wrapped envelope. I knew that enveloped anywhere. Her brother was the most amazing artist and growing up I used to beg him to draw me pictures. In fact, I have a collection of them in a binder. His drawings were always really special, especially since he added the touch of having them delivered in a gold envelope a few years ago.

My best friend enveloped me in a hug, that lasted so long, I think the guard was beginning to get nervous that she was secretly slipping me contraband. Jason spoke first.
"Can I give my girlfriend a hug now too?"

Macy started laughing, and I was surprised he told her. I wanted to be the one, but when you were locked in the can I guess your options were limited. She stepped aside graciously and allowed him to hug me before shoving the envelope into my hands.
"Open it! I have waited for him to finish this piece for days. You know how Elliot is about his "masterpieces."
"Okay, okay," and motioned for us all to sit down.

I slowly began to unravel the cord and opened the enveloped. I pulled the edge back, grabbed the familiar paper, and pulled it out. I was speechless.

It was a beautifully intricate drawing of myself in a chair, surrounded in a massive library filled with books of all colors and sizes. The library looked similar to the one in Beauty and the Beast, which I always adored. Elliot knew this. The chair he drew me in was a velvety red color, which I had also expressed that I wanted in my library in my home one day. The best part of the picture was the way Elliot drew me.

I looked so peaceful without a worry or care in the world. It was an absolutely stunning picture. I would cherish it forever, and one day have it framed. I turned to Macy.
"Thank you. I know Elliot drew it, but you were the mastermind behind this. I absolutely adore it. You're amazing."

"Oh please, you deserve it. You're a saint! Being in here, while the real killer walks around free. Just wait until I prove it…" she said looked angry.

"Please don't burden yourself with their issues Macy. I have faith that it will all come out at trial," and forced a smile.

She returned the smile, and I passed the picture to Jason who had not yet gotten a chance to see it. He was as taken aback as I was, fawning over all the little details that Elliot hand drew.

"Wow Mace, Avery is right. Elliot is crazy talented! Have you ever submitted his work to an art contest or something? If not, you should!"

She laughed. "Okay, don't ever say that around my brother. We don't need his head getting bigger than it already is."

We all bust out into laughter. These were the times that made the hard days in here worth it. I was able to be with my friends, not in the way I wanted to be, but still. Bright side, remember?

Jason decided it was an appropriate time to present me with the gift he got for me. It was beautifully wrapped in a gold and silver paper. I gasped when I saw the front of the box. Pandora. I opened it slowly, and there was the most beautiful ring in there.

It was a silver ring with a gorgeously cut emerald in the middle. It was stunning. I became nervous. I didn't want to be proposed to in a prison visiting room. I looked over at Macy whose eyes were not watering. I laughed; she was an even bigger baby than I was. I looked over at Jason who was smiling. He grabbed the box and removed the ring.

"I can see you panicking, stop. I'm not proposing, but I will someday. I know times are not the greatest right now, but I am always here for you. Forever, I want you to know that. This ring is simply a symbol of that."

He placed the ring on my finger and kissed my knuckles. Macy just about screamed. She grabbed my hand and was checking out the cut and style of the ring. Obviously thoroughly impressed, she patted Jason on the back and said, "Well done."

I had to admit, having something beautiful to look at in such a dismal place like this, would make it slightly easier. Knowing it was Jason who gave it to me, and his promise he made with it, made all the difference in the world. I wasn't sure if I was able to have jewelry- my guess was no so I quickly palmed the ring and kept it hidden.

We spent the next hour talking about anything and everything that was going on in their lives until visiting hours were over, and my friends had to go. I had received a call that my lawyer decided to come tomorrow instead. Apparently, he felt it best if he came the day before the trial started.

I ate dinner with my new prison friend that night, and it was nice to have the company. She told me about her family, and how she would be up for parole soon. She still has never divulged the reason of her incarceration to me, but I wasn't one to pry. Well, I was but not when it was concerning a potentially dangerous inmate.

I headed to my cell after eating and decided that some reading would be the best way to keep the trial off my mind. The lawyer was coming tomorrow, so I would think about it then. I picked up an aged copy of Harry Potter and the Sorcerer's Stone and began to read it for the third time.

I became lost in the world of wizarding and felt myself mumble something about Slytherin before I drifted off to sleep. I woke up to the door unlocking, as I always did. I had an appointment with my lawyer. This ought to be a blast. I pulled my hair back into a bun and headed over. He was already waiting with what seemed like a mountain of paperwork. He actually seemed upbeat, which should be a good sign. I sat down.

"What's the good news?"

"I have a really good feeling we can win this case."

"And how would that be?"

"We will call Erica on the stand. I'll go at her hard, and hopefully shatter her testimony? They may still have the shirt, but I want to see if I have a shot at discrediting her statement."

"That may work, but it won't be easy."

"Oh, I'm looking forward to that."

My lawyer loved a challenge, and he said that this was a challenge like he had never faced before in all his years. Oh, that was comforting. He assured me that he knew just how to crack a witness, especially one that was lying. He wanted to know anything that he would be able to use against her. Her miscarriage with Brandon sprang to mind, but I was never that cruel. Even if she was exceptionally horrible lately.

"Nope, nothing. I'm sorry but she's not a very forthcoming person."

"That's okay, I will figure something out. Now don't stress please, I think we have a good shot. Get some rest and take it easy today. It's a big day tomorrow."

That was easier said than done, but I thanked him, and headed to my cell. I just wanted to push my troubles to the side and get lost in a great book. I picked up where I started yesterday.

By the time I looked up, it was time to eat. I headed down and sat next to my friend. She still had never told me her name. "Tomorrow is the big day. I can't believe it's only been a week since I've been in here."

"You would think time would pass quicker, but it's much slower than anyone realizes. About the trial, I know it will go well. I don't want to see you back here, understand?"

"Understood," and I hugged her thanking her for the comfort she has brought me in a trying time.

"Anytime."

I finished my meal and said what I hoped what would my last goodbye to my prison friend. I guess we were going to start with Erica on the stand first. The prosecutor would ask his questions, and then my lawyer would cross examine her.

I laid in bed that night but couldn't even find the energy to read a single chapter of the book. I was much too nervous. This could easily go a much different way than both my attorney and I anticipated. I had to be prepared for the very real possibility that the jury would convict me, and I would go to prison.

It was such a terrifying thought to realize your hands was in the life of some people who didn't know you. They didn't know your character, or all the good you had done in your life. All they would know would be the lies the prosecutor fed them tomorrow. I wonder if the prosecutor thought I was innocent. If she did, and still chose to pursue this case, then I had to question her ethics.

By a miracle of God, I was able to sleep. I surprised myself when I woke up that morning without having a single nightmare that night. I did feel mentally drained but that was a daily occurrence now.

I was transported to the courthouse, and that is where I was allowed to change into the clothes my mom bought for me. They wouldn't allow Macy to bring them to the jail that day, so we had to wait. I put on the outfit and found myself pleasantly surprised. My mom picked out a light blue blouse, and a paid of formal dress pants paired with black heels. She also dug my blue headband I used to wear in the fourth grade, probably as a means to make me look more innocent, but all it was doing was giving me a blistering headache.

It took about ten minutes of arguing with my mom to get her to agree to let me ditch the headband. This woman was nuts! I was eternally grateful for her support. I don't know how I would have gotten through this week without the help of her, Macy, and Jason- my saviors.

I guess this was the hard part. My lawyer met my mother and I in the room and we prepped over what he was going to say. It all seemed reasonable, and I was optimistic that Erica would admit to all her lies.

It was time, and we headed into the courtroom. I was expecting Erica to already be waiting on the stand, but to my surprise she wasn't.

I spotted Jason slipping in the door and taking a seat next to my mom- but no sign of Macy. Maybe she was running late. The judge emerged from her chambers and called the court to order. She began introductions and the lawyers followed. She then instructed them to call their first witness. The prosecutor said,
"We call Erica Parsons to the stand."

I turned my head and watched my ex friend glide up to the witness stand. She was unsurprisingly dressed head to toe in the most decadent outfits, all designer of course paired with a pearl necklace.

We made eye contact momentarily, but she was the one to break the stare first.
Her prosecutor began.
"Miss Parsons, you were at the cabin the weekend in question with your friends, correct?"
"That is correct."
"Can you tell me who you were there with?"
"Sure. I was there with Brandon, Macy, Joey, Jason, and Avery."
"Just to clarify, can you point to the Avery you are speaking about."
She pointed at me and looked away.

"Let the record show that the witness identified the defendant, Avery Grant. Can you describe what you heard the night in question, Erica?"

"We had all had a lot to drink, and Brandon and Macy were helped upstairs to the bedrooms by Jason and Avery."

"What about you?"

"Well Joey and I were falling asleep on the couch."

"I see, but you woke up at some point in the night yes?"

"Yeah, Joey and I both woke up and heard Avery and Brandon arguing."

"What were they arguing about?"

"I couldn't hear, but she sounded angry."

"Okay, nothing more your honor."

I glanced over at my attorney, unsure if this was a good or bad sign. He adjusted his tie and winked at me. Oh, this was a good sign. He began his cross examination.

"Miss Parsons, you said you heard Avery arguing with Brandon. Is that correct?"

"Yeah, both Joey and I heard them."

"I see. You didn't see anything? The loveseat that you apparently fell asleep on was directly facing the front door. So, you heard them, but didn't see them? Were your eyes closed?"

"My eyes weren't closed; they were arguing upstairs."

"So, in your intoxicated state you were still able to hear someone arguing upstairs?"

"I wasn't that drunk, and yes, I was. They were really loud."

"Loud enough to wake Macy? She was in the bedroom next to Brandon and heard nothing, yet you who was downstairs heard everything. Does that make sense?"

"I don't know, all I know is what I heard."

"You said they were loud; did you make out what they were saying?"

"No, I already told you. I couldn't understand them."

"Surely you could. They were "really loud" as you put it. At any point, did you see them come downstairs?"

"No, I think I fell asleep."

"What time was that?"

"I don't know. Maybe 4 a.m.? Yeah it was 4:15, I remember looking at my phone."

"There's a small issue with that, Erica. Brandon was killed at approximately 2-3 in the morning that day. How could you have heard Avery and Brandon arguing if he was apparently already dead?"

She went silent for a minute, before answering.

"I maybe had the times wrong."

"Or you're lying, which is it? Tell us the truth Erica. It's a crime to lie on the stand."

Erica burst into tears.

"So, what if I lied? All I did was help get a warrant, she was the one caught with the bloody shirt! She's guilty!"

There was a round of gasps from the jury, before the judge banged her gavel, "Order!"

My attorney was first to speak.

"Your honor, following the admission of a false statement, I move to dismiss all charges."

The prosecutor spoke next,

"There is still the bloody shirt we found in her closet."

The judge sided with the prosecutor and ruled to throw out Erica and Joey's joint statement given to police. The trial was now resting solely on the t shirt found.

We were granted an hour recess before resuming. That gave us an hour to explain how the shirt used in the murder was found in my closet and clear my name. How hard could it be?

# **Chapter 15**

We headed into my attorney's office to collect ourselves and develop a strong explanation for the shirt. The problem was I didn't have an explanation. I had no clue how it got there. I knew it was Joey, but I had absolutely no proof. He knew exactly where we kept the spare key, and when I was home or not. He wasn't my biggest fan lately, and I knew he wouldn't stick his neck out for me. Hell, he and Erica practically laid mine out for the guillotine.

I couldn't help but think of Brandon in that moment, and how absolutely disgusted he would be at the thought of all of us lying, scheming, and deliberately trying to hurt one another, it wasn't right.

I decided that maybe my original plan of trying to convince the jury of my innocence would be my best bet, and my lawyer agreed. All we had to do was convince one.

My mom and Jason were allowed to stay with us during the duration of the "recess". It brought comfort to me and eased my stress immensely. I just wished Macy could have made it. Nevertheless, Jason reached out and pulled me in his arms but was stopped by my mom.

"I get her first! Baby, you're doing so great out there. I just know they will see the truth, I just know it," and gave me a comforting squeeze.

She planted a kiss on my head and stepped to the side allowing Jason to embrace me. The support that was so effortlessly given to me made all the difference throughout the entirety of this nightmare. If I didn't have them, I would have given up and accepted my fate a while ago.

The remainder of the hour was spent talking to my mom and Jason about what we planned to do when I got out, while my lawyer was preparing. I knew I wouldn't be getting out but wanted to see them optimistic one last time. I didn't have the heart to ruin their hopes. I just didn't.

Before I knew it, the hour was up, and it was time to explain to the court how a piece of evidence from the murder I didn't commit, found its way into my closet.

We headed inside and I was racked with nerves but hid it well. I made sure to look at the jury, all of them, when entering just like my lawyer said. Apparently, I was next on the stand.

"Okay, recess is over. Defense, call your witness."

"We call Avery Grant to the stand, your honor."

I slowly stood up and walked over to the stand. I felt as if I was going to fall on my face at any moment, but by the Grace of God, made it without a single slip.

"State your name for the record please."

"Avery Grant."

My defense continued, "Where were you at the time Brandon was murdered?"

"I was asleep on the couch, next to Jason."

"At any time that night, did you wake up?"

"I didn't open my eyes, but I remember hearing whispers and then the jingle of Brandon's car keys."

"So, you were semi-conscious, but never opened your eyes. Is that correct?"

"That's correct."

"Miss Grant, did you kill Brandon Fuller?"

I looked out at the crowd, and spotted Brandon's mom. I answered confidently.

"I did not."

"Do you know who did?"

"I don't know, but maybe it was the same person who lied about hearing Brandon and I argue."

The prosecution objected, and before the judge could open her mouth to speak, my lawyer spoke first.

"Withdrawn," and he added, "No further questions, your honor."

I began to panic. No further questions? How was anybody supposed to believe I was innocent after that? It was the most basic line of questioning.

The judge told the prosecution to begin their cross examination.

"Miss Grant, you said you were semi-conscious, and heard the jingle of Brandon's car keys. However, you said that you were a heavy sleeper. How did you remember something like that?"

"I am a heavy sleeper, and I didn't remember it originally. I went to a hypnotherapist after the incident, and she helped me remember."

"By help you remember, you mean creating a false story?"

"It is not a false story. I could never have killed Brandon. In fact, the only reason I am in this situation is because I underestimated people who I thought were mt friends."

"I see," and began to grab a bag of what I assumed was the shirt.

She turned to the jury and held up a bright yellow sweatshirt. I gasped. It was mine. Except I wasn't wearing it that night, Macy was.

My head was spinning out of control. This didn't make sense. Maybe there was a mistake, maybe Erica borrowed the sweater. I refused to believe my best friend was capable of murder, or even planting the evidence on me. She would never do something like this to me. Were Joey, Erica, and Macy all on it together? Macy would provide the evidence, and Erica and Joey would pair it with a false statement to get me imprisoned?

"Miss Grant, I asked you a question."

"I'm sorry, what was it?"

"Is this your sweater?"

"It is, but I wasn't wearing it that night."

"Who was?"

I scanned the crowd but saw no Macy- only Jason who looked just as in shock as I was. He knew exactly what Macy was wearing that night.

"My friend Macy. I let her borrow it."

"So, you conveniently let your friend borrow a sweater on the night it was worn to kill Brandon Fuller?"

I choked out a small, "Yyes."

"I have a hard time believing that Miss Grant. Tell me, do you lie often?"

Instead of answering her, I decided this would be my last chance to prove my innocence to th jury. I was not going to jail for this. I turned to the jury.

"I never would have killed my friend; you have to believe me. Brandon was everything to me!" I mournfully sobbed.

The prosecutor redirected.

"Would a friend do this?" and held up a photo of Brandon. It was taken when they found him. He looked unrecognizable under all that blood. I was going to be sick.

I couldn't help it, when I leaned over the witness stand and blew chunks. I was so ridiculously squeamish. They called a small "recess" while the janitor came in and cleaned up the mess I made. We were in the lawyer's office.

"Listens to me. That was my shirt, but MACY was wearing it the night Brandon was killed. I swear."

Jason chimed in with, "It's true. She was wearing it all night."

My lawyer decided it best if he went to speak to the prosecution alone. He wasn't even gone for five minutes before he was back, looking especially defeated.

"She didn't want to drop the charges. She still thinks your guilty, Avery. She offered a plea deal, to 5 years with chance of parole. I declined."

"Good! Five years for a crime I didn't commit. This is insane!"

"Has anyone been able to contact Macy?" Jason quipped.

"Nobody call her. I want to talk to her myself when I get out. Wait, I have a plan- call the prosecutor down here. I need to talk to her alone."

About ten minutes later, the prosecutor walked in and her and I stepped off to the side. I told her about my plan, and she agreed to drop the charges. We all returned to the courtroom.

The judge spoke. "Prosecutor, you may continue cross examination."

"There will be no need your honor. The DA's office is withdrawing the second-degree murder charges against Miss Grant."

The judge said, "Wise choice," and followed it with, "Court is adjourned. Avery Grant, you are released." And banged her gavel.

I was so excited. I could taste the freedom. I would no longer have to spend my days confined in a cell. I was free.

Before I could properly celebrate, the prosecutor pulled me aside. She said,

"Remember the stipulation. We have a deal."

"I would never. I'll be in contact when I have it."

She walked off leaving me to my smug attorney, and Jason and my mother. I don't know why he looked so smug; I was the one who got the charges dropped. We were all screaming, crying, and jumping around. I looked to the back of the courtroom in time to see Joey and Macy. They looked almost remorseful. I didn't care. In fact, I walked right past them with so much of a glance their way.

"What do you want to do first Aves? Pizza at Johnny's?"

"I actually have something I need to do first, mom. Raincheck?"

"Well, okay," she grumbled.

Jason pulled me to the side. "What's going on? What deal did you make?"

"Don't worry about it. I have it under control. I need a ride though."

I said my goodbyes to my mom and thanked my lawyer for all his hard work in my case. He did help me out a lot. Jason and I got into his car, and I rolled the window all the way down. I had only been in jail for a week, but I couldn't get enough of the feel of fresh air on my face.

He asked where we were going, and I gave him the address. He turned to me and said, "Macy's house?"

"Just trust me, Jason."

And with that being said, he continued on his way to her house. I had to mentally prepare myself for what I was about to do. Her house was about thirty minutes away considering the courthouse was a bit out of town.

The drive gave me time to think, and Jason left me to relish in the silence.

I was trying to piece it together now that I knew who killed Brandon. Macy. I still couldn't believe it. Why would she do that? How? Did she plan to wear my sweater while doing that, or was it a happy coincidence when she realized she could pin it on me? The girl who brought me a commissioned hand drawn picture in jail was a killer. Worse, she tried to make me seem like one too. I really hoped she had the answers that I so desperately needed to hear.

"You okay, Aves? Pretty quiet over there."

"Just thinking, about Macy, about everything."

"I know. I can't believe she did, what the hell is going on?"

"I have no clue. Hey, did she know that the evidence would be presented today?"

"Yeah, your attorney told all of us."

"That makes a lot of sense why she wasn't there then. She knew I would recognize the shirt, you too."

We both fell into a comfortable silence. Our heads were spinning. To have someone you have known your whole life, turn out to be such a sinister and twisted person breaks your heart.

I felt like I didn't know this person anymore. I needed to get answers- why she did it. That begs the question of Joey and Erica though- why did they lie? Were they that mad at me they wanted me to go to prison? Did they find out it was Macy and conspire with her? My little group of six was slowly growing smaller as I realized half of them were cold blooded and had bad intentions.

Brandon was killed by one his best friends. Did they get in a fight? Brandon was killed right in the front of the house, while we were all sleeping peacefully and blissfully ignorant inside. Did he ask for help? My heart was breaking.

I decided to call Brandon's mom, and apologize for everything that happened. She picked up on the first ring.

"Oh Avery, I am so sorry dear. I heard that the DA's office dropped the charges. I never once thought it was you."

"I'm sorry that you had to go through that. It has been a trying week. Don't worry, I will get justice for Brandon. I promise you."

"No Avery, let the police handle it. I don't want you to get mixed up in this again."

"Don't worry, Mrs. Fuller. It's handled." I hung up the phone.

I turned to Jason after, and he looked fully confused. I watched as he pulled into a Starbucks and ordered a venti black coffee for me.

"I just figured that you needed some liquid strength for whatever you are about to do. Plus, they don't give coffee in prison, do they?"
I laughed, "Not the good stuff," and followed with a, "Thanks Jason."

It felt so good to be outside of those walls, with Jason, happy. I was so ready to just be happy after all of this. The trial had worked in my favor. I was ready to begin my new life, with Jason. I had to take care of something first. I sipped on my coffee during the remaining ten-minute drive. My stomach was starting to do somersaults. I had to be strong though. This had to be convincing.

I was fully prepared to go in Macy's house, and put on the show of my life. I planned to tell her that they threw out the whole case after Erica admitted to lying on the stand. I wouldn't let her know that I had seen the shirt, or that I had a recorder in my pocket.

We pulled up to the house a few minutes later. I was so nervous, but Jason took my hand, looked me in the eyes, and said, "You got this."
He added, "Please be careful Aves. I'll be right here."

I stepped out of the car and didn't see any cars in the driveway besides Macy's blue Honda civic. Oh boy.
I knocked on the door, and to my surprise it swung open.
"Hello," I said as I stepped inside.
"I was expecting you."

I turned to the left and saw Macy sitting in the recliner, eyes bloodshot, and what had to be a very large kitchen knife in her hand.
"They showed you the shirt, didn't they?"

# **Chapter 16**

"Macy, what is going on?"
"They showed you, didn't they?"

"They did. I didn't wear the sweater that night Macy."

"Of course, you didn't. You let me wear it, and once I realized- it was the perfect opportunity to frame you."

"You planned to kill Brandon?"

"Oh no, he was simply collateral."

I was so taken aback. I didn't even recognize the girl sitting in front of me. How could she ever refer to Brandon as collateral? She was messed up beyond repair. She continued,

"I always liked him; you know."

"Brandon?"

"No not Brandon, you half-wit, Jason."

"What does this have to do with Jason, Macy?"

"He was never supposed to be with you. It was him and I that always had the connection. Until little Miss Avery had to walk in and steal him like she always did," she laughed coldly.

I never stole Jason from her. They were in the same class and were friends before she introduced him to me. If I had known she had feelings for him, I would have never gotten together with him.

"You're not making any sense Macy."

She laughed, as she twirled the blade. "How's this for making sense? I was so sick and tired of you and Jason constantly flaunting your relationship, throwing it in my face- so I hatched a plan."

"The funny thing is, I see now that you two belong together. You see, you're both the same. Two righteous people who never make any mistakes. I needed Jason to be with me, just once. I knew he would see that he had feelings for me."

"What do you mean?"

"Jason was too noble to ever cheat on his girlfriend, so he needed a little…encouragement."

"What the hell did you do?"

"Oh, calm down. It was nothing that would hurt him. I knew he wasn't much of a drinker, so I crushed a Rohypnol tablet and sprinkled it in his drink. That was all it took."

"You drugged Jason?!"

"He needed to see that I was better for him than you ever were," she continued. "But when the morning came around, Noble Jason was back."

"Do you even have the tiniest bit of remorse for what you did? You intentionally split Jason and I up, you drugged him, you set me up for murder and killed Brandon!"

"Hmmm you're also forgetting about the cockroaches, and the wet suitcase," she laughed without humor in her voice.

My best friend hated me. She had gone out of her way to intentionally sabotage me time after time, and then turned around and smiled to my face. She wanted to ruin my life. She took Brandon's life.

"I don't care about me, why did you kill Brandon?"

"Ah, that was unfortunate, wasn't it? Brandon found out about what I did to Jason, and said he was going to tell. I couldn't let that happen, now could I? I wasn't as drunk as everyone thought, in fact I waited until you and Jason fell asleep, woke Brandon up, and convinced him I wanted to talk in the car," she continued, "He was always so naïve, wasn't he?"

"Is that why you went back the night after? You left something behind?"

"Well no, but I wasn't sure. I didn't find anything anyways."

"I can't believe you. You're a monster."

"I'm a monster? How about the girl who went around from friend to friend accusing them of murder? You never did ask the right questions, or the right person. You're pathetic."

"I WAS TRYING TO HELP MY FRIEND! That's something that you don't know ANYTHING about."

All she did was laugh. It was lacking humor, yet full of malice. My head felt like it was about to explode. I didn't know this person sitting in front of me. Macy was a monster.

"Why do you hate me so much? I mean all these plans revolve around me, right?"

"You think you're the greatest person in the world Avery, but you're not. You're selfish, rarely think about others, and I was sick to death of living in your shadow. You're mistaken. I don't want your life; I just want to ruin it. Just curious, have you ever known what it felt like to be on the outside? To never felt like you belong. Wait, let me answer that for you, no, because you always get whatever you want."

"Is this a joke? I just got out of prison! Erica and Joey hate me! Brandon is dead. What makes you think my life is so perfect?"

She said nothing, but instead started humming. She palmed the knife and pressed it into the arm of the chair slowly twisting it, adding more pressure until it began to tear a whole, she was crazy. "Did you get enough evidence on me for the prosecutor," and motioned to my leg where the recorder had become easily visible. Damn it.

"I did actually, and you're going to prison for a long time," I said as I got up to leave.

"I'm not going to prison, and you should really sit down, or you'll be leaving in a body bag. Don't you want to hear how I killed Brandon?"

"I really don't."

"Oh, you're squeamish right. Oh well. It was rather quick actually. I asked him to get something in the back seat. I hit him from behind, which knocked him out. I lifted up his legs and piled them in, so he was laying on his back. I just hit him, again, and again until I felt better."

"Jesus, you're sick. He was our FRIEND."

"He was your friend; I never really felt a part of that group."

"Aw, Macy got her feelings hurt. Did you ever consider that the reason you didn't fit in is because you're a sociopath? It doesn't give you the right to go around killing people. You deserve to spend the rest of your life rotting in that cell."

"But I won't. I also told you to sit down."

Just then the door swung open, and Jason stepped inside. He spoke first.

"What the hell is going on? Avery, you okay?"

Macy continued, "Look how sweet. Jason coming to protect Avery. So predictable. Take a seat Jason, join us. I was just telling Avery how I killed Brandon."

He looked at me, at her, and at the knife in her hands. He took a seat next to me.

"Macy, you don't have to do this," Jason pleaded.

She disregarded Jason and looked at me.

"Jason missed our earlier discussion. Did you want to fill him in or should I?

"Macy, don't," I pleaded. She continued regardless.

"I drugged you. That night we slept together. Turns out you were right about only having one drink, although with a little Rohypnol, that's all it takes."

He turned towards me, and Macy, open mouthed and obviously in shock.

"What's wrong, Jason? Cat got your tongue?"

"You hateful bitch! How could you ever think Jason could love someone like you? You're a waste of space. If I could trade, I'd let you take Brandon's place," I spit with contempt dripping from my voice.

She looked as if I had slapped her, but quickly recovered. "Anyways, I was about to tell Avery all about how I hid the shirt in her house. Funny thing is, I hadn't expected Joey and Erica to be the ones to call. I was actually going to do it. Weird, how people will react once you have upset them. Avery has become a champ at it recently."

"I can't believe I'm still entertaining you. You're worthless. I don't want to ever see you again," I said as I stood to walk out. Jason got up with me and grabbed my hand before I felt myself hit hard from behind.

I fell forward and rolled onto my back just in time to see Jason shove Macy onto the floor. She dropped the knife that she had been holding, and they were struggling. I needed to make it over to the knife. My body wouldn't move, and my head began to throb as I felt the burning sensation of a million tiny pinpricks. I could hear them fighting and tried to look, but my eyes felt so incredibly heavy. My vision was blurring. I needed to help Jason.

I reached out and found the leg of the iron coffee table. I latched my hand onto it and with mustered up all the strength I had left and pulled myself upright. I immediately felt dizzy and took a second to steady myself. Once my vision had refocused, I saw Macy with her fingertips reaching for the knife. Jason was on top of her, hands around her throat.

"Jason, stop!" He turned to me, and that gave her all the leverage she needed. She grabbed the glass bowl to the right of the chair and brought it down on his head. The glass shattered and Jason fell to the side. Oh god, what had I done. She stood up, knife in hand, and looked at me.

"Do you see? You're the one always getting people hurt. You're the problem."

She started towards me, and I stood in in one swift movement and kicked my left leg out towards her foot. I succeeded in catching her off guard, and she fell, grabbing me in the process. Once again, she dropped the knife and it fell several feet from us. I couldn't let her get on top of me.

I pushed her off and started crawling towards the knife. The carpet felt like sandpaper, and my head was throbbing uncontrollably. This hurt so bad. Right when I felt like I was about to reach it, Macy yanked my foot and pulled my whole body a couple feet back. I hit my head on the edge of the coffee table, and my vision started going black.

I heard Jason's voice, and then Macy's scream followed by a loud bang.
"Avery, wake up," I could feel Jason shaking me and the warmth of his breath on my skin.

I peeled open my eyes, and most of the pain subsided, but I felt dizzy. I would be lucky if I didn't have a concussion. I looked around and saw that Macy was lying flat on the ground. Jason began to help pull me up and out of curiosity I looked around but spotted no knife. Jason helped me onto the couch and went off to the hallway to call the police. I reminded him that she might need an ambulance.

I looked back at Macy, and she looked... twisted. Her body was at a completely different angle than before. I stood up and peeked my head into the hallway.
"Jason, did you grab the knife? I haven't seen it."
"No why would you- look out!"

He reached out to grab me, but it was too late. I felt pain slice through my midsection and looked down to see that blood was beginning to pool and seep through my shirt. I fell to the ground, and Jason dropped his phone and caught me before I hit my head once more.

The door slammed, and I realized Macy had run out. Jason tried to keep me talking and refused to let me fall asleep even though I was so incredibly tired. I felt my eyes growing heavier and heavier, until I began to hear sirens and fire trucks.

I remember being lifted and placed on a soft bed- which I assume would be the stretcher. All at once, I had a flurry of people circling me, sticking me, taking my heart rate, and I felt an oxygen mask get placed on my nose and mouth. They shined a bright light in my eyes, and I could barely make out what they were saying.

I watched as a policeman pulled Jason to the side, but he insisted on being with me on the way to the hospital. He climbed in beside me as they loaded me into the ambulance. There were two EMT's taking turns applying pressure while one was checking my vitals, I think.

I didn't feel as if I had much strength, but made out the words, "Call my mom."

The ride felt short, and before I knew it, the doors opened up and my mom was standing right there. I had never felt so safe in my life, then in the moment.

Doctors rushed out to pull me inside and I watched as they made Jason and my mother stay behind.

"She has a stab wound, deep. Her concussion is also pretty bad. She has been falling in and out of consciousness," the paramedic explained to the doctor.

Had I? I couldn't figure it out because everything faded to black.

# **Chapter 17**

I could hear a murmur of voices but wasn't fully able to make out that they were saying. And then it was dark.

I woke up later, in a hospital bed with tubes coming out of everywhere. I saw my mom asleep in the spare bed, and spotted Jason in the hallway on the phone, looking really angry.

I opened my mouth to speak but was surprised when nothing came out. My throat felt really dry, and I reached for the water cup on the side table. I couldn't reach it, so I twisted my side and, "Ow!" I screamed.

My mom's eyes shot open and Jason came rushing in through the door.

"Avery what happened? Did you rip your stitches?"

I was confused and lifted up my shirt. Sure enough, she was right. I have to have gotten at least thirty stitches. Jesus.

"Avery, I'm so glad you're okay. You had me worried there," Jason said as he lifted my hand and kissed my knuckles.

I couldn't help but smile. I was in a lot of pain, but I was really happy. Oh god, Macy.

"What happened to Macy?"

The mood of the room suddenly shifted.

"That girl should be in prison. In fact, I have to let the detectives know you're awake. They will need your statement, love," and my mom left the room.

"Jason? Tell me."

"She fled the scene Aves. We have policemen on the lookout for her. They apparently put out an APB and are tracking her credit card activity. They will find her."

"How could she do this to me? How could Macy try and kill me? What did I do to make her hate me?"

"Don't. It's nothing you did. There is something *wrong* with Macy. I'm with your mom on this one. She deserves to be behind bars plus a week for the hell you went through."

I remembered the recorder and slipped my hand into my pocket but felt nothing. I checked the other and it was empty too.

"Jason, the recorder!"

"…is right here." The prosecutor walked through the door clutching the recorder.

"I am so sorry for what you have gone through. Rest assured, Macy will go away for a very long time. It is just a matter of finding her now. But please, get some rest. You have been through a lot," and with that she squeezed my hand and left the room.

I couldn't be mad at her. She was only doing her job. In fact, I found myself being actually grateful. If she hadn't taken a chance on me and allowed me to prove my innocence then Macy would still be walking free able bodied to hurt another person and I would be behind bars. Another person I was grateful for was Jason. If he wasn't there, she probably would have killed me. I owed him my life.

I reached out and squeezed Jason's hand.

"Thank you… for everything. I mean it. If you weren't there today, I might have died."

"Don't thank me, I was glad I was there. If something had happened to you… because of her…" he started to tear up.

"But it didn't. Well it did, but I'll live," I said with a laugh.

Jason smiled, and I continued,

"Macy?"

"They haven't found her yet," Jason said disheartingly.

"Have you been in contact with police?"

"I actually have. In fact, I was just on the phone with Detective Greene. It is no longer in his jurisdiction, but he assured me he was personally investigating. He feels horrible about what happened."

"…and he shouldn't. Macy was very convincing- even had me going for a bit there."

"Hey, don't be hard on yourself. The only person here to blame is Macy… and me."

"Jason, you heard her. You were *drugged*. The only person to blame is her. Don't forget that."

He sat on the edge of my bed and held my hand. These past two weeks have been absolutely unimaginable. I wouldn't have gotten through it without Jason. What would I do about Macy? How do I move forward now? I know who killed Brandon, and yet I didn't feel any better. I guess it was time to finally face his death.

Ever since he died, I emerged myself in investigating as a way to not deal with the way I really felt. I had done it all my life, and I was just now starting to realize that it wasn't exactly effective.

Brandon and his mom were always so good to me. My heart broke for his mother, and all that she has been through these past few weeks. I so badly wanted to fix everything for her, but I couldn't. I also would do anything to bring Brandon back. Macy was a destructive and toxic person. I wondered at what point she had shifted from the sweet girl I grew up with to a monster capable of murdering someone.

Jason squeezed me hand and said, "I bet you want coffee. The hospital doesn't have the best stuff, but I'm sure anything will do right now," and he walked out. I laid my head down.

I saw someone coming in out of the corner of my eye and thought maybe Jason forgot his wallet.

"Hey Jason, forget something?" I sat up. To my surprise, it wasn't Jason, but Erica and Joey.

"Got any more lies you want to tell? I'm sure you can find a police officer right outside the door. Maybe they can even handcuff me to the bed. Although, I did get stabbed."

They both looked remorseful, but something I had learned recently is that emotions could be faked. Macy perfected the art of doing that.

"Avery, we are so incredibly sorry. Look, we were so hurt by your accusations, and we thought it was only fair if you felt as if you were under the microscope too. We didn't think you did it but thought that Detective Greene getting the warrant would scare you a little. But when they found the shirt, Avery we thought you really did it. It looked bad. We thought you killed Brandon, and so we agreed to keep our story up, if that's what it took to put you away," she rambled on.

Joey continued, "When Jason told us that it was really Macy, and what she did to you- we had to rush over here. At the end of the day, you're not just our friend- you're family Avery. We will be here for you no matter what."

"Where were you when I was sitting in a jail cell for a crime I didn't commit? Where were you when I wasn't able to properly mourn my friend because I was too busy trying to prove my innocence?"

They flinched as if my words had cut right through them.

"We are so sorry. We can never tell you enough," they both said.

I stayed silent for a moment and allowed my thoughts to process. As angry as I still was, I couldn't afford to lose any more friends. There were two I was never getting back, well one I didn't necessarily want back, but still. What they did was hurtful, but nothing compared to the pain Macy has inflicted on this entire group. She was truly a "wolf in sheep's clothing."

"I'm sorry too. The way I went about the whole thing was wrong, and it led to forcing you to talk about something that was private Erica."

"No, actually it was good. Talking about it helped. I have held that secret for so long, that even just telling one person felt like a boulder had been lifted off my shoulders. I am able to come to terms with it, and finally properly mourn the baby I lost. I do have some comfort in that I know Brandon and our child are together."

"Come here... both of you," I said with arms outstretched for a hug.

They both rushed in with full speed.

"Careful! You don't want to break her," Jason said coming in with two extra large coffees. This man got me.

Erica and Joey both backed off my aching wound slowly, and hugged Jason. I think we all had been very distant from each other lately, and it hadn't been helpful for any of us. Joey broke away from the hug and came over to me. He sat on the edge of the bed. "I'm sorry Avery, I never should have believed you were capable of something like this. But Macy... I can't believe it. The fact that she hurt you too- you could have died Avery. I can't even imagine... and if we were still on the outs- I never would have forgiven myself."
"Joey, Macy is a disgusting person. I know what kind of person you are, believe it or not. Through everything, I think a small part of me knew that you didn't hate me. It was just a confusing time. The things you said though..."
"I know. I have kicked myself everyday over what I said to you outside your house. Like you said, Brandon's death has messed with my head in ways I didn't even think were possible. Avery, I want you to know... I don't find you disgusting. In fact, you're probably one of the kindest, and noble people I have ever met."

He squeezed my hand, and I smiled. My friend was back. It was true, that Brandon's death had messed with all of us. The detective's findings early on had a lot of us pointing the finger at each other, well mostly me anyways. I think it may have made us all stronger in a way. Brandon would be proud of us. I wish he were here to see us, one last time.

Brandon's mom walked in. She was carrying my favorite flowers, yellow roses.
"Oh god dear. How are you? I heard. I'm so glad you're okay," she said as she sobbed.
"I am a lot more durable than I gave myself credit for apparently. Hey, please don't cry Mrs. Fuller. I am okay. I'm sorry- about everything."
"Why? I talked to your mom outside. She told me what you did with the recorder. It is just a matter of finding this girl now, and once they do- it's a guaranteed life sentence. She may not have premeditated Brandon's murder, but she did kill him. She also tried to kill you, and apparently... drugged Jason? What a messed-up girl." She continued,

"I know you're and need rest. Your mom said you had a really bad concussion. I just needed to come and say thank you. Thank you for finding Brandon's true killer." She turned around.

"And thank you. I am sorry I ever accused you. Thank you for sharing yours and Brandon's story with me," she said as she hugged Erica.

Oh. I guess Erica truly was opening up about her miscarriage. I guess a part of me was glad that I played some role in her being able to feel able to talk about it, and not suffer in silence. I am glad that Erica has someone to lean on and has found comfort in Joey. Those two were made for each other.

Brandon's mom left, and it was just my friends and me. I was so glad that we were all safe, and together. This nightmare was finally over. Erica and Joey moved to the side and looked nervous.

"What's going on?"

"We have some news."

Jason moved to my side, and we started, fixated on Joey and Erica waiting for them to spill.

"We're getting married," Erica said, and she revealed her ring that she had been hiding in her purse.

She moved closer to me so I could get a closer look. It was so beautiful. It was a gaudy diamond that was pear shaped and enclosed with a circle of diamonds around it. The band was also encrusted with more diamonds. It was a ring fit for someone with Erica's taste. It must have cost a fortune.

"Wow! I'm so happy for you guys. Rather soon though, no?"

"Yes, it is. Erica may have started having feelings for me only recently, but I have loved her for a long time. If anything, the past few weeks have shown us just how short life is, and how we can't waste it."

Erica and Joey kissed, and I felt so overjoyed for my best friends. Jason was grinning ear to ear, and I could tell that he was excited for them as much as I was.

My mom walked in, saw the ring, and also burst into a round of congratulations for the happy couple, and then hugs.

After she finished staring at the beautiful ring, she seemed to remember the reason she came in.

"Avery, the police are here to take your statement."

Just then, two uniformed officers came in, as well as Detective Greene.

"Detective Greene, I thought this wasn't your jurisdiction any longer."

"It isn't, but I had to make sure you were okay. I feel awful."

"And like I told Jason; you don't need to feel awful. Macy was very clever at deceiving people. Apparently, she had been doing it to me for years."

He looked sympathetic for a moment, and continued, "These two officers are here from your local precinct to take your statement. I don't know if Jason told you, but I have personally been privately investigating since this happened."

"And?"

"Well I have been tracking her whereabouts, and she only used her credit card once. We went to where it had been used, but she was already gone."

"Where did she use it?"

"Avery, she purchased a firearm."

# Chapter 18

I was in shock. A gun? I immediately felt this pit in my stomach followed by a wave of nausea. Macy was a danger- to herself and to all of us. Did she buy the gun to hurt herself? Or was it to hurt me? I couldn't figure out her motives, because up until today I didn't really know her. I finally found the words to speak.

"Do I need to be scared for my life?"

"At this point, I don't know what her motives are, but she does have a very clear hatred for you. You need to be careful, and always watch your surroundings. My hope is that we find her before anything else can happen. Your police department has an officer stationed right outside your door," Detective Greene assured me.

With that being said, he turned and went to fill the other officers in. Jason came to my side followed by Erica, and Joey. They all were all curious about what happened with the detective.

"Detective Greene has been tracking Macy's financials. They got one hit off the credit card."

"Great! Did they find her?" Jason wondered.

"No, they didn't find her. But they went to the store where it was used. Guys, she bought a gun."

They were all taken aback, and Jason begin to get angry.

"Why the hell does she need a gun? She's insane if she thinks she is getting anywhere near you again Avery. She has caused enough damage for a lifetime."

"Jason's right. We're not going to let her hurt you again," Joey said, and Erica nodded in agreeance.

"I don't think she's coming after me guys. Yeah, she stabbed me, but maybe she realized what she did. I worry that she bought the gun to use it on herself."

"While that would take care of a lot of our problems, I highly doubt it. Macy has proven something time and time again- she doesn't feel remorse. She doesn't care about the people she hurts, including the girl who has been by her side her whole life."

I thought about what Jason said for a moment, he was right. From drugging Jason, to sabotaging me, and killing Brandon- she proved that she didn't feel remorse or guilt for everything she did. And now this- I was laying in a hospital bed nursing a killer concussion with thirty brand new stitches where she stabbed me. Once I began to piece together the timeline of events, I could see just how bad she was beginning to get.

It all started seven months ago when she drugged my boyfriend in order to get him to sleep with her, which was apart of a larger plan to steal him from me, and then put cockroaches in my bed, drenched my suitcase, and killed our friend when he found out her secret.

In addition to that, she tried to get me sentenced for the murder. She was a monster. I was just glad that I finally knew exactly who she was. Now I could know what to expect. As much as I gave my friends a different idea, I knew the gun was bought to kill me. She had to of known I survived, and I was sure that infuriated her. It was okay, because when she came, I would be waiting.

Macy would definitely bide her time until I got out of the hospital. She wouldn't risk anything with a cop right outside my door. Although these days, I never knew what she was willing to risk or what she was truly capable of. She did underestimate me though. I wouldn't go down without a fight.

"Avery?"

"Sorry guys, I think I'm a little tired. Could we visit a little later, my head is throbbing? And can you send my mom in?"

They all agreed that rest would be best for me but promised to return in the morning with some of the finest coffee our little town had to offer. My mom came in shortly later.

"Mom, what did the doctor say? How long until I can go home?"

"Well you need to stay here another day at least so they can keep an eye on your concussion. It was really bad Avery," she said as she started to tear up.

"Mom, please don't cry. I'm okay, I promise. I am just ready to get home."

"Well, let me talk to the doctor and I'll see what I can do," and she planted a kiss on my head.

And just like that, I was left alone to deal with my thoughts. I did really feel exhausted. In fact, I had been through so much these past few weeks that I think it was just now starting to catch up to me. I remembered my coffee and took a big sip. Oh god, Jason was right. It's disgusting, but it will have to do. I need my energy.

I remembered that Macy and I had linked our phones to share our locations with each other at all times. Out of curiosity, I pulled up our messages and hit the tab to check her location.

I didn't recognize where she was, but it looked like thirty minutes outside of town. She was hiding. I called Detective Greene. "Hi, I just remembered that Macy and I share our locations with each other. I tracked her phone, and I have an address for you."
"I appreciate your effort, but we already tracked her phone and came to the location. She isn't here, just left her phone… and a note."
"What did the note say?"
"I'll take a picture and send it to you- it's quite long. But Avery, please get some rest. We are handling this," he said and hung up.

No less than a minute later, my phone buzzed. It was a picture of the note. It was long, just like he said. It read:

This note is for Avery. The one who stole everything I wanted in life and threw me to the side. The knife was a warning shot. I heard that you lived, and that you are resting comfortably at the hospital with an officer stationed right outside your door. Enjoy the rest Aves. Truth is, you can't stay there forever. Sometime in the next few days, you'll go home. Might want to hide your spare key under the planter or get a new one. I might have already made copies. Did they tell you I got a gun? I've been practicing. Well, I have to go- a life on the run can be draining. See you soon, Aves.
Love, Mace.

Oh god, she was insane. She was not going to stop until she killed me- or I killed her. This note would freak my friends, and especially my mom out. I couldn't show it to them. I saved the picture to my gallery and deleted the message. All I could do is get as much rest as I could safely in the hospital, and then be ready when she came, like she said. The thing is, even without the note I knew Macy would come back eventually. She had so much hate towards me and stabbing me wasn't an accident. She thought I would die- she *wanted* me to die. She was absolutely psychotic.

Why just me? I wonder why she didn't have any resentment towards Jason. He chose to pick me time and time again, even after they slept together. Knowing the way Macy operated now, it was likely that she felt that was also my fault. Maybe she thought she could kill me like she killed Brandon, and then no one would be left to stand in her way of getting Jason- just like she has always wanted.

Thinking about Macy was making my head spin. I really did need to rest. The coffee didn't just taste bad, but it gave me zero energy. I laid my head on the pillow my mom brought from home and was out like a light.

I woke up to my mom holding a croissant from my favorite bakery. Oh god, I hated hospital food even more than I despised hospital coffee.

"You have no idea how good that smells!"

"Here, enjoys love. So, I talked to the doctor and you will be here for two more days."

"I thought it was only one?"

"Well, he just feels that two days will maximize your recovery time. I am glad though. I will admit that having you here, safe and protected, makes me feel better."

"Mom, I don't think Macy will come after me. The cops even said that she probably did it because she felt cornered."

"Don't forget Avery that she killed Brandon. She isn't someone who made a couple mistakes. She chose to kill someone and *chose* to try and kill you. Do not make excuses for her," my mom warned.

"I'm not! I swear," I said as I nibbled on my warm butter croissant.

"Well, I brought your laptop so you could watch some Netflix, and a book if you wanted to read," she said as she kissed my head, and went out in the hallway.

I should have known my mom would see through my efforts to try and ease her worry about Macy. Everyone had more than likely already heard the tape. To hear the malice and coldness in her voice as she casually described the details of Brandon's gruesome murder was unnerving to say the least. It definitely changes your perspective on a person, even one that you had know your whole life. It certainly changed mine. Point is, they knew what she was capable of. She wanted me. She wanted to hurt me. It was always me. It broke my heart that Brandon was a casualty in this war brewing silently between Macy and me.

I decided to text Jason. It read: Did you want to come visit? I could use the company.

It was a few minutes later when he replied. He said, "Of course. I'm on my way."

I decided to maybe try and look slightly presentable. I pressed the nurse's button, as I was a "high fall risk" and wasn't allowed to get out of the bed without help. The nurse came running in almost immediately and I asked if she could walk me to the bathroom so I could freshen up. I brushed my hair, my teeth, and even found concealer in my purse.

Once I felt slightly presentable, I got back into bed. I saw that my mom had also snagged me a coffee from the bakery. I took a long, savory sip. Honestly, I could stop anytime I wanted. I just didn't want to.

I slowly sipped on my coffee, as I waited for Jason and killed time just scrolling through my social media. My page was flooded with "Get Well", and "Thinking of you!" comments from people I had maybe exchanged two words with my whole life. It didn't matter, it was nice. After everything I had been through, some niceties were welcomed with open arms, regardless of who they came from.

My mom came back in and informed me that she had been speaking with the police. There were still no leads. They had a few people claim they "spotted" her, but unfortunately nothing had panned out. I wasn't worried. I knew she wouldn't risk being seen until she was coming for me. I had a few days.

"That was my coffee, by the way," my mom said while laughing.

"Well, you left it in my possession, and now that I've started, I hope you know I am not giving it back. But don't worry, they have a great selection of coffee brewed from the finest beans downstairs," I chuckled.

"You're funny. Are you friends coming back anytime today?"

"I texted Jason to come visit. He's on his way, but he is taking a little bit longer than I expected."

"Don't worry, I am sure he will be here soon," my mom assured me.

Just then the uniformed officer that was guarding my door stepped into the room.

"Do you guys know a Jason Carter?"

"Yeah, he's my friend. He is on his way over."

"I'm sorry, but I just got a message over the radio. He's been in an accident."

# **<u>Chapter 19</u>**

I felt like my heart had been ripped out of my chest. It was all my fault. I asked him to come here. If he had stayed at home, none of this would have happened and Jason would be safe.

I couldn't find the words to speak. Thankfully, I didn't have to.

"Is he okay? What in the hell happened?" my mother inquired.

The detective didn't have information on how it happened, but that Jason was being taken by ambulance to the same hospital as myself. He is not doing well but expected to live. Thank god.

I called Joey and Erica. I felt they should know that Jason was injured. It would help Jason if he saw his friends when he got here. What if he needed surgery? How bad was it? I couldn't bear let alone stomach the thought of losing him. At this point, he was the only thing keeping me strong.

I couldn't even think of Macy right now. She was worthless, and at the moment Jason and his health superseded everything. She, and her revenge fantasy would have to be left on the back burner.

I said a prayer for my friend.

"Avery, I am going to go wait for Jason to arrive and call his mom if they haven't already. Will you be okay by yourself for a bit?"

"Please, mom. You know I love the quiet. Please make sure Jason is okay for me."

"Of course," and with that she sprinted out.

With the exception of a slight speeding issue, Jason was a good- no great driver. I don't understand how he got in an accident, especially one that warranted a hospital trip. At this point, I didn't even know the extent of his injuries. It really felt like one thing after another. It was hard to look on the bright side, when it truly felt like this was a game of poker, and I keep getting dealt a bad hand.

Erica and Joey arrived within twenty minutes, and we all waited in my room to hear more information on Jason. I was a patient myself, so I didn't really have a choice.

I knew the likelihood of Jason having his phone near him, let alone be using it, was slim. I texted him anyways. It was simply, and sweet. It read: I love you. I hope you're okay. Call or text when you get checked out.

I wondered if he would need surgery. I wish someone would give me an update, because sitting around waiting did nothing for my nerves and I was supposed to be recovering! I was a mess.

Just then my mom sent me a text: Got downstairs right as his ambulance was pulling up and found his mom. We saw Jason, from the looks of it a broken leg, and bruised face. He will be okay, love you.

Thank god it wasn't more serious, but a broken leg? My god, it must have been some accident. I relayed the news to my equally worried friends, and together we all breathed a sigh of relief. It would honestly prove a miracle if one of us could go the remainder of the week without getting injured.

Jason sent me a text: They are fixing up my leg now. I am okay, thank you. I have to admit this wasn't what I pictured when I decided to come hang out. I will talk to you more in person, but the weirdest thing happened. I came up behind someone, and my brakes gave out completely. That's why I crashed. Odd.

That was weird. Especially since I personally accompanied Jason less than a year ago to get his brakes replaced. We had been having exceptionally rainy weather lately, and maybe it had eroded his brakes earlier than expected. I was grateful that he had been driving on the streets and not going seventy-five down the freeway.

Just then, my doctor came in to do a progress check on me. He said I seemed to be improving, but that the rest shouldn't stop when I was discharged from the hospital. Dr. Brandt took a look at my stitches, and said they seemed to be on the path to healing nicely and noted that I was lucky that she didn't hit an inch or two higher. Yeah, because that was exactly how I felt after almost dying from a stab wound- lucky.

Jason texted and let me know he had been checked into a room, but that he wouldn't likely be staying the night. I wanted desperately to see him, so I had Erica ask the nurse for a wheelchair and for permission for Joey and her to take me downstairs to see Jason. The nurse happily obliged.

It took forever to get me out of bed, into the wheelchair and out the door. Jason was only two floors below me, and we took the elevator, naturally. We got into the room, and I was relieved to see that Jason was not as injured as I originally would have thought. The broken leg was evident and would obviously take some time to heal.

His face didn't look bruised, but rather slightly red and a bit swollen. I had no doubt it would fester into a bruise. I was glad he was not badly injured.

I had Joey and Erica roll me over to him. I couldn't fully twist myself out of my chair to attempt to hug him, but hand holding was always our solace. I reached out and our hands found one another. Jason was my peace in this crazy thing we call life.

His mom and mine were in the room, fretting over their "broken" babies, as they so poetically put it. I didn't feel broken, even though I should. Mentally, physically I felt stronger than ever. I had been put through the absolute ringer the past few weeks and it gave me the stability I so desperately craved.

For what felt like forever, we sat and talked- Jason, Erica, Joey, our moms, and me. It felt good to be surrounded by people you love and who love you, especially when you are hurting.

"Jason please elaborate about the brakes. We just got them changed not too long ago," I asked.

"I don't know guys. It was really the strangest thing. I was cruising, not going fast, and the light went from yellow and then to red in a matter of seconds. I didn't slam on the brakes, but I definitely tested them out. Instead of taking a while to stop or slowing down slower than usual, they just didn't work. I felt no resistance, and I practically pushed the pedal into the floor," Jason explained.

"Is there any way we can have a mechanic look at your car? If your brakes are going to shit that soon, we definitely need a refund."

"I think we can, but a refund is not something I am worried about right now."

We were all in agreeance that the brakes would have to wait. All that was important was that Jason and I healed without any necessary stress. I think Jason's doctor said he would be out within the day or early tomorrow morning, and I had another one-and-a-half-day sentence here.

I remembered Erica and Joey's wedding and grew really excited. I knew Erica always dreamed of being a bride and having a glamorous and over the top wedding. Joey was in for a lot.

To take my mind off Jason and his broken leg, and the resurfacing Macy, I asked Erica about her wedding plans. That was all it took because she then launched into a thirty-minute tirade about dresses, and flowers, and cake. I was almost sorry I asked. I was just so happy to be not fighting with my friends, that I would've allowed her to talk for another few hours.

However, the nurse came into the room and advised me to head back to mine. Like they kept telling me, "I needed my rest." They were all like broken records around here. It grew quite tiring.

Joey and Erica decided it best to retire home for the night but promised they would return the following day. Jason's mom opted to take the extra bed and sleep in his room for the night.

My mom rolled my back up to my penthouse suite, or room 506 as they call it. She waited until we got situated before laying it on me heavy.

"So, we haven't had a chance to talk because everything has been so absolutely crazy. I don't miss things though. You and Jason?"

"Yeah. It has kind of been going on since the trip, but the revelation of Macy's only highlighted what we felt all along- that we never should have broken up," I explained.

"Well, I will be the first to say that I am glad. I always thought he was right for you. He makes you laugh, Avery, and that makes me feel good."

"I think he just may be the love of my life."

"I hope so baby," and kissed my head.

Suddenly, we were both exhausted. Similar to Jason's mom, my mom had them roll in an extra bed for her again and she decided to stay with me at the hospital. I think a part of her was still worried for my safety despite an armed man at the door, but a part of her also might have been scared to be alone at the house.

Macy was so depraved, and I think it struck fear in all of us. At least, it did. I wasn't scared of her anymore. The shock of all she had done was wearing off and sinking in, and I was just beginning to understand how twisted she was. I hated her, more than I had ever hated anyone before. Knowing that she still felt she had unfinished business with me struck a fire in me I had never felt before.

I knew she would be coming for me the minute I got home. I expected it. I welcomed it. If she ever tried to hurt me, or anyone else I loved ever again, I would kill her.

I fell asleep thinking of all the ways I could avenge Brandon. Macy deserved to pay for what she did, and she would- in due time.

When I awoke the next morning, my mom was gone like always. She had to have her coffee first thing in the morning. Once you meet her, there really is no doubt who my mother is. We were the same person.

She came skipping into my room, with another croissant and a coffee from my most beloved bakery. She was humming and looked over the moon.

"Are we in a good mood today… at 8 a.m.?" I checked my watch.

"We sure are my love. The doctor changed your release date around. You will be able to leave tonight around 8 p.m. Unfortunately, that means you will have to spend one more day here but that's at least twelve hours before you were scheduled to go home and that, my dear, is a cause for celebration!"

My mother always got excited about the littlest of things. I must admit, getting out of this hospital room and back into my bed did sound extremely appealing. My only worry was that I had not regained enough of my strength to be fully prepared for the inevitable showoff with Macy.

She gave me my coffee and pastry and headed out to get an update on Jason. God, I loved that woman.

Just then, an officer came into the room. He was easily identifiable as a police officer but didn't look familiar.

"Hi, can I help you?"

"Hi, I investigate car accidents. One of your friends Joey called me about an accident your other friend Jason was in. I reported my findings to him, and a woman named Erica earlier, and they wanted me to come by and give you my report and findings as well."

"Well, what did you find?"

"The reason your friend Jason's brakes weren't working… is because they had been cut."

Macy.

# **Chapter 20**

Jason's brakes were cut. There was no other person capable of doing something like this other than our friendly neighborhood murderer, Macy. I had wondered if she hated Jason as much as she apparently did me, but I guess I have found my answer. Macy hated both of us, and I guess it was enough for her to want us dead. I knew what she had in store for me, though.

The investigator said it was Erica and Joey that hired him. I knew that he already told them his findings, but I had to talk to them. I had to find out if they told Jason what they found out.

I sent out a quick group text to Erica and Joey. It read: Just talked to the investigator. Did you tell Jason?

I heard a phone chime.

"No, we didn't", Joey said as he and Erica walked into my room.

"Why not? He needs to know who tried to sabotage him. He needs to watch out for himself. Obviously, I am not the only one that Macy held a grudge against, and I don't want him to get hurt again."

"We wanted to wait until he was discharged," Erica explained.

That made sense, I guess. Jason would be safe as long as he was in the hospital. Macy may be borderline psychotic, but she wasn't stupid. She wouldn't try to kill either of us again until she had full access to us. That reminded me about Macy's threatening letter.

"Hey Joey, do me a favor? Can you please change the locks on my house, and give me the copy? I don't want to leave the copy in the usual spot. I have a feeling Macy knows where it is."

"Uh, sure, yeah of course. I'll do it tonight, actually."

"Thank you- I owe you. And Joey? Please be discreet."

He nodded in agreement and took Erica's hand and they left.

I wondered if when all of this was over, if I would finally feel that my head had stopped spinning. I had felt like a mess since Brandon was killed, and these past two weeks have been nothing short of eventful. In fact, that was an understatement. Knowing who Brandon's killer was gave me a sense of peace and allowed me to properly grieve for my friend. Apart of me feels responsible, especially since Macy's chilling confession.

Brandon found out a secret and was going to tell me, and that's exactly why he was killed. Brandon died because of his loyalty to me. Jason almost died, because he loved me, and Macy hated that. Macy may have orchestrated a lot of these events, but I was the true cause. I was the one who created all this pain and was the root of everyone's suffering. Maybe, Macy was right to hate me so much. I hated me.

I knew that if Macy were to come for me again, I would be ready. She wanted me dead. I would do everything in my power to stop her, and I was not going to let her hurt anyone else at my expense. This needed to be put to an end. Normally, knowing Macy I would've guessed that she would come to my house the day I got home. She was a creature of habit. But now, I feel like she will use my "knowledge" of her to her advantage. Maybe, she'll surprise me, and make me frantic waiting for her to show.

I needed a gun.

I had already been in a physical battle with Macy, and I lost. If she was going to be bringing a gun to this fight, I needed to be prepared. I did not want to base my chances of survival on getting the gun away from her. It would never work.

Along with all my other feelings, I can't help but to be so angry. Macy claims she had lost everything because of me, but that simply isn't true. I can't believe that she has ever felt like an "outsider". In fact, she seemed to fit into the group so seamlessly. She has mastered this persona that she wears around us. She had all of us fooled. I hated her with such a passion, and I was almost happy for her to come for me. I wanted her dead, and the satisfaction of doing so would be everything to me.

I had begun to let my thoughts turn dark, and to turn into someone capable of murder. Up until recently, I could have never had thought I could be capable of taking someone else's life. The truth is, I never want to. The thing is, if I want to beat Macy at her own game she has crafted, then I need to think like her.

That's the only way this would ever be over. I needed to win- whether that would be to get her in jail or kill her.

I drifted off to sleep consumed by my thoughts of rage, revenge, and loss.

I awoke the next morning knowing that I would be getting to go home today. If Jason's doctor was true to his word, he would be going home today as well- just a lot earlier than me. I texted: Hey, are you getting released today? Miss you, hope the leg is feeling okay. Xox.

Jason: Yes, I am being evaluated as we speak, and then the discharge papers need to be filled out. Doctor says leg should heal fine, but I got a pair of awesome crutches, so there's that. How are you?

Me: I'm fine, just a little stir crazy. Want to go home. I must admit, I am jealous of your crutches. All I got was stitches and a killer concussion.

Jason: Yeah, but you're lucky that was all you had. Macy was after you. I was just a loser who forgot to change his brakes.

I forgot Jason didn't know. Erica and Joey wanted to wait until Jason was released to tell him. I guess that was now, and I wanted to be the one to break it to him.

Me: Can you hobble your way up here? Need to talk.

I didn't get a reply from Jason, so I figured that he probably was already on his way home. I opted to call him later and break the news, until I saw him hobbling into my room.

"Hey Aves, you called, I came," he said with a laugh.

"Hey Jason, I would hug you, but the stitches don't allow for optimal mobility, unfortunately. I am glad you're here though."

"Of course, Avery. What's up? You seemed like you really needed to talk."

"Sit. So, the story about your brakes not working seemed off, and we were all worried about you."

"Who's we?"

"Erica, Joey, and I. They hired an investigator who took a look at your car. Jason, the brakes were cut."

Jason took a long deep breath, closed his eyes and went silent. I hesitated to speak, for fear of what I would end up saying. So, we sat, in a long eerie silence. Jason finally spoke after what seemed like hours.

"Macy?"

"We think so. Look, I am telling you because you're leaving to go back home, and I need you to be careful Jason. We know what she's capable of and now we know that she wants to not only hurt me, but you."

"Not hurt. She obviously wants to kill us."

"I know."

So, we sat there, both staring at the other and deciding what we should do. What could we do? Call the police, have them station a car, be escorted everywhere? It was all useless, and all it did was delay the inevitable. It was probably a good time to tell Jason about the note. The one that specifically says Macy was coming to kill me. I took one look at his already fragile state and opted against it.

No, this would have to be something I did for myself. I couldn't allow anyone else to get hurt in the crossfire. This was my mistake, and I would fix it before it affected anyone else, I loved.

"So, just be careful, I guess?"

"Sounds like a plan. I'll be here for the rest of the day, but I meant what I said Jason. You have to be careful, because I don't know what her plan is."

That was a lie, but it was one that would benefit everyone. I just needed to keep this charade up for a while longer.

Jason scooted over to me and kissed me. It wasn't long, but it was successful in bringing the relief I so desperately needed.

Jason brought out such a peace in me, that I secretly wished we could stay in this moment forever. I more than anything wanted to begin our life together, blissfully ignorant and happy.

He said that his mom was waiting for him, and off he went. I wasn't alone for long, because my mom came in with the usual: a flaky buttery croissant, and a steaming cup of coffee- my favorites. I couldn't imagine anything else better to kick off the day of discharge from the hospital. I was ready to be home.

My mom stretched out on the bed next to me, with her laptop she brought from the house. She planned to spend the say with me, and work from the hospital.

"Hey Avery, why did Joey change the locks at 2 this morning? He scared me half to death," my mom questioned.

"I asked him to. It will help me feel a little bit safer especially with Macy not being caught yet."

"I suppose you're right. It has had me feeling a bit on edge."

And with that, she continued on to do her work. I laid in bed, consumed by my thoughts. I needed to work out a plan, and fast. Joey may have changed the locks, but that wouldn't keep Macy away.

I doubt she would come tonight, but for her it might seem like the safer bet. More people are asleep, and there are less witnesses. I wondered what her plan was. Did she think she could come, kill me, and go off living her life? Or did she know she would go to jail, and wanted to just get me out of the way before that? I was going to stress myself out wondering how her demented mind worked. So, I pushed it to the back of my mind.

I killed time the rest of the day by bouncing from one social media app to another. Before I knew it, it was time to go and I had accomplished nothing in terms of a plan for Macy. I guess I would be forced to wing it.

My mom signed the discharge papers, and we collected all of our things. I sent a quick text to Jason letting him know I was leaving and reminded him again to be careful and watch his back. I sent Erica a text letting her know I was discharged and thanked her for everything. I decided to call Joey.

"Hey Joey, I'm being discharged now. Mom and I were going to pick up dinner on the way so we will be about thirty minutes. Can we come over to get the keys then?"

"Sure Avery, no problem. See you soon. Oh, and be careful," Joey warned.

I was so tired of being told to be careful and warning it myself. I would relish in the day when my previous best friend would be locked away for the rest of her life... or spend eternity in the ground- either one would be good with me at this point.

I did a seemingly good job of convincing not only my mother, but the police that I wasn't scared and didn't think Macy would be coming after me. The police knew about the note, but I was pretty sure Detective Greene didn't tell them he sent me a picture.

Like we decided, we stopped and picking up some Thai food on the way. Nothing like comfort food to wait out a murderer.

We got home and stopped over at Joey's quickly to retrieve the keys. I thanked him again and let him know I would see him in the morning for coffee.

My mom and I used our brand-new keys to unlock the house. We sat down and enjoyed a meal in front of the tv- one of our favorite pastimes together. My mom decided to call it a night a few hours later and bounded up the stairs to bed. I was tired too but could feel the adrenaline pumping through my veins.

I laid down in bed, determined to make myself go to sleep regardless. My phone started to ring, but it was distant. Damn it, I left it downstairs.

I pulled myself out from under my warm and cozy covers to get my phone. I reached the bottom step and felt the punishing cold breeze coming from outside. The door was wide open. I knew I locked everything.

I grabbed my phone which was on the table. It was some random number, so I declined the call and went to close the front door- again. Just as I shut it, I heard a gun being cocked, and felt the cold metal barrel push against the back of my head.

"Well, hello Avery. Glad to see you've made a full recovery."

"Hello to you too, Macy."

# **Chapter 21**

"I will go anywhere you want me to go Macy. Let's please not do this here," I pleaded with my former best friend.

"Of course, you will. I'm the one with the gun after all. Leave the phone. Let's go," Macy said, as she began pushing me out the door.

"Where are we going?"

Macy pulled out a roll of duct tape from the waistband of her jeans. She held the gun on me as she ripped a piece of with her teeth, and then taped my hands together. She led me to her car and put me in the backseat. She instructed me to lie down, so no one would see me.

She loaded herself into the front seat. I wished more than anything I had the ability to speak, because I was sure that I would be able to talk her down if I tried...

*Who was I kidding? She was crazy.*

So, I laid there, in the all too familiar backseat. Despite everything that had happened, this still didn't feel real. I was forced to accept that the Macy I knew, or thought I knew, wasn't the person who was driving this car- or maybe she was. Maybe this was the person who Macy was her whole life, and I was too blind to see it.

I knew she would have no trouble killing me. After all, she killed Brandon- and just for knowing something he shouldn't. Macy lacked remorse, and basic human decency. Like I said, she was a monster. The only way I could get out of this unscathed, was to beat her at her own game. All Macy knew was violence.

I laid in the back seat, eyes focused on the window, trying to catch a glimpse of anything to give me the tiniest inkling of where we were headed. The way I was positioned, I was only able to see the streetlights and trees, as we drove past them in a blur. I couldn't tell exactly, but it didn't feel as if we were moving too fast. That made sense.

If Macy were to drive like a crazy person, she would surely get pulled over. One little flashlight pointed in my direction would be all it would take for her ass to get hauled off to prison.

*Please pull her over.*

No such luck, as we kept driving for what felt like forever. If I was guessing, we had maybe been in the car for thirty or forty minutes. That meant she was taking me out of town. I had left my phone, so if anyone noticed I was missing they were screwed on trying to track my phone. No, I would have to get out of this myself.

I knew Macy would come tonight. Which is why I had my mom's old hunting knife tucked right into my left sock. I just prayed Macy didn't find it.

"We're here," Macy said in a singsong voice.

*God, she made me sick.*

Macy parked, and all lights I saw while driving were gone. The place we had arrived at was as close to pitch black as you could get.

She got out of the car at lightning speed and opened my door. She pulled me out towards her by my shoulders, and my hair got snagged on the seatbelt. Rather than unhook it, she just pulled me harder, resulting in a chunk of my hair being torn out.
*Bitch.*

I suppose that was in my best interest- DNA being left behind. Not that it really mattered, as I already knew myself that help wouldn't come, and I was my only chance.

I had to fight like hell. I was out of the car and started to look around. My suspicions were right, there was no light here. It was pitch-black and took my eyes a moment to adjust. It looked like an abandoned building, that had been improperly cared for. She began to walk me towards the building, and through the front threshold.

I took every chance I had to examine the areas around me. The silver paint was chipped off the walls, and the building had a faint gas smell. I wondered if there was a fire here.

There was hardly any furniture in here, besides a curved office desk that looked like it had been put through the ringer. I noticed burn marks printed on the sides of it and knew that my earlier deductions proved true.
*Did she plan to shoot me?*
"What are you thinking about, Aves? Awfully quiet…"

I tried to speak, but remembered the tape plastered across my lips.

She began to laugh, obviously relishing in my discomfort. We turned into a room, which had nothing in it, but a chair with rope around the legs of it. I could tell this was set up before Macy came and got me. There was a small lantern in the center of the room, with a video camera lying on the floor next to it.
*What the hell was this?*
"Take a seat, Aves." Macy said as she shoved me towards the chair,

I sat down, and she immediately came over to bend down and fasten the rope to my legs. Naturally, she tightened it as tight and did the whole process as rough as she could manage. When she was finally pleased with her handiwork, she took a step back and admired.

She was really enjoying this, as much as I'm sure I would enjoy seeing her being shoved in the back of a squad car.

"I brought you here for a reason…" Macy explained.

"You see… you were supposed to die that day. But you didn't. I knew that I had to fix my mistake- to kill you. But then I got the most brilliant idea. What if I staged it to look like a suicide? What if I filmed you confessing to all the horrible things you did?"

She walked over and ripped the tape off of my mouth- not very kindly either. Obviously, she was curious as to what I thought of her heinous agenda.

"That's the best you got? Are you thick or are you forgetting that Jason watched you stab me? You will never get off scot free regardless of what you do. There are a lot of people betting on that, and your downfall."

She looked angry for a moment and started towards me, but then stopped in her tracks. She was figuring out her next move.

"Well, we will never know if it will actually work unless we try, right?" she said with a sinister smile.

*I wanted to slap that look right off her lying face.*

"Your plan will never work. There is no way in hell I would ever lie for you. You deserve to pay for everything you did," I said harshly.

She raised the gun and pointed it directly in between my eyes.

"You don't exactly have a choice, do you? You are forgetting that this story doesn't have a happy ending… for you at least."

She walked out of the room, and I heard things being moved around. She reemerged with a tall stool. She moved the stool directly across from me, about five feet away. She grabbed the video camera and set it gently on top.

"So, here's what we are going to do. You're going to sit here and confess to everything about the murder."

"What exactly do I say?"

"Well, you will start by telling them that you grew tired of Brandon and wanted him out. You will confess to pulling him out of his bed that night and convincing him to go to the car with you and talk. You will admit to taking that brick from the edge of the grass, and smashing him over the skull with it, then driving to the location."

"One problem with that Mace. Where is the brick?"

"I, well you, threw it in the river by the house. You need to state that you also wiped off the handle of the car," she explained as if this was a completely normal thing to do.

I reminded myself that the only way I was going to get out of this was by playing her game- and beating her at it.

"Okay, let's get this damn thing started."

"That's the attitude! Now look somber and remorseful," Macy said, as she turned on the camera.

There were so many things wrong with her plan that would without a doubt not convince any of the police officers of my guilt. How did I tie myself to the chair, and then also start the camera without moving? Macy was absolutely clueless, but I guess when revenge is your sole motivation, logic goes right out the window.

I stared straight at the camera, ready for this all to be over. I began.

"My name is Avery Grant. I killed Brandon Fuller, and it's because of this that I have chosen to take my own life. Since the murder, and the accusation of my dear friend Macy, I see just how much pain and suffering I have caused. The guilt is overwhelming, and I simply cannot take another day of this personal hell. The night Brandon was murdered, I was angry with him. I lured him out of his bed and convinced him to talk to me in the car. He was opening the backseat door, when I hit him in the head with a brick- over and over again."

I stopped. While fake, this confession made my stomach churn. How she could go about murder and discussing it so nonchalantly, I would never understand.

I looked at Macy, and she gave me a look that said, "Keep going," and held up the gun as a reminder of what would happen if I didn't.

I opened my mouth to continue spewing whatever line of bullshit she had fed me. I saw motion behind her, and felt my chest expand with hope, but knew not to give it away.

I continued my speech, and saw Jason coming up behind Macy. I tried not to make it obvious, and I was successful. Jason swung, and Macy fell. He was holding a similar stool that I assumed he found outside with the others. Macy had dropped like a ton of bricks, but I knew from experience that she did have an excellent track record of getting up, so I urged Jason to hurry.

"I am so glad to see you. How did you find us?"

"I put a tracker on Macy's car. Joey texted me saying he saw that your door was wide open and was worried. I checked, and when I saw that her car was idle thirty minutes south of the city, I knew something was wrong."

"Did you call the police?"

"No, but I will. I wanted to make sure you were okay first. You are my only priority," Jason said.

I felt my heart swell, but dismissed my warm feelings due to the dire hostage situation I found myself stuck in. Jason was always saving me. He finished untying me and I walked over to turn off the video camera. I grabbed the gun off the floor and heard Jason cry followed by a loud bang.

I turned, and found Jason lying on the floor seemingly unconscious. I hoped he wasn't, for my sake. Macy looked at me, her face dripping with contempt.

"You're not going to shoot me, are you? You and I both know you don't have it in you, you never have."

It felt like I was floating outside of my body, as I watched myself pull the trigger. She dropped to the floor. I stood over her as I watched the blood pool in her chest. My finger was still resting on the trigger, my head in a battle with my heart. I wanted to fire again. To get justice for Brandon. A voice in the back of my head urged me not too, reminding me that there was too much violence and death already. I felt a mental hand pull me back, no a physical hand. Jason.

His forehead was bleeding from a slight cut, but he would be okay.

"Don't do it Avery. She deserves to rot in prison. Death is too easy for her."

Jason was right. I wasn't a killer, and I wouldn't allow her to turn me into one. Jason pulled out his phone and dialed the cops, Detective Greene, and my mother.

Within five minutes I heard a number of sirens going off, followed by loud shouting and police rushing in the building. They had an ambulance waiting for Macy, and Jason. They loaded Macy onto the stretcher, and an officer walked up and connected handcuffs on her to the metal railing. I have never felt more satisfied in my entire life.

My mother rushed over to me and enveloped me in a tight hug.

"Don't you ever do something that stupid again!"

"Need I remind you, she kidnapped me!" I said laughing through tears.

Detective Greene walked over to the two of us.

"Avery, I must say you just may have a future in police work. They have her in custody now, and I can assure you she will be going to prison for a very long time. Are you okay?"

"Well, my stitches feel like they ripped open, but knowing she will pay for Brandon's death makes it all the better. By the way, she tossed the brick into the river by the rental home."

Detective Greene laughed. He patted my back and apologized for everything we had been through.

I made sure the police officers took the video tape with them. There was nothing but my false confession really on there, but I wanted every ounce of evidence against Macy to be taken into custody. I felt something sharp, and realized I still had the knife. I decided to keep that tidbit of information to myself and return it to my mom's things discreetly later.

The EMT's stitched Jason's forehead up, and he ended up only needing six stitches which paled in comparison to my thirty something, but who was counting?

"We did it, huh?" Jason said smiling.

"I would say we make a great team, but that sounds cheesy. So, I'll just do this instead," and I leaned in and kissed Jason. This time it wasn't a chaste kiss, but rather a passionate one that ignited that familiar fire all over my body.

We pulled away, fully knowing that we had an audience. The EMT cleared Jason but told him to follow up in a week to get the stitches removed. I wanted to go home, and rest my head on my pillow, but no such luck.

In fact, Jason and I were due at the precinct to give our formal statements to not only the police, but the District Attorney. It was what they called an open and shut case. Needless to say, I didn't want to run the risk of taking any chances.

I was sure Joey was worried and had probably given Erica a heads up. I texted them:

Hey guys, it's me. The night has been nothing short of insane, but Macy has been formally arrested. I left her a nice little bullet to remember me by. Meet up for coffee tomorrow? We have a lot to discuss.

I found my mother again, and together her, Jason and I got into the car and headed to the station. It was finally over.

# **Chapter 22**

The drive to the police station was strangely calm. I felt at ease knowing that this nightmare was finally at its end. The district attorney had her evidence, and now the police department had Macy. The fact that she held me at gunpoint, while trying to force a confession out of me, probably tacked on a few more charges.

Macy had morphed into a person who I was no longer interested in knowing. I wanted to cut all ties with her, now and forever. However, this version of Macy probably didn't care if I no longer wanted to be associated with her or not- she was emotionless. Besides, she wanted me dead. There was a great satisfaction of knowing that she would be sitting in prison. while I was allowed to freely live my life.

We arrived at the station, and the officers whisked Jason and I away to take our formal statements. I gave them the run down of all the events of the last few hours. I confirmed what they already knew- that I shot Macy. Jason corroborated with me when I told the officers that she was charging me when I fired. It wasn't true, but a little lie never hurt anybody. She deserved that bullet and much more.

When we emerged from the room, we found both of our mothers sitting in the waiting area for us. Jason's mom made a beeline for me surprisingly. She leaned into my ear, and said, "Thank you, for saving my son."

*Did I save him?*

I didn't feel as if I have saved him, but rather the other way around. The truth is, I had completely forgotten about the knife in my sock, and probably would have died at the hands of Macy and her gun.

Jason rushed in and saved me, never mind the dire consequences if he had failed. I loved him. I squeezed his mother back and reminded her that Jason was the true hero. It was as if she only just realized her son was there too, because she turned and nearly crushed him with her tight hug.

My mom's arms found mine, and soon enough all four of us were a bunch of hugging fools.

I felt myself visibly relax. I was so glad to have this whole thing over. It has been a smorgasbord of different emotions since the day that Brandon went missing. Throughout the ups and downs of this "journey", if you will, I have had one emotion that remained the entire time. Sadness. I had been so caught up in trying to solve his case and figure out which one of my friends did it, but every time I was able to catch a breath, I found myself overcome with an aching heart. I missed my friend, and I didn't imagine the day I would ever stop.

*I'm so sorry Brandon.*

"You guys want to go get something to eat?" my mom propositioned.

"No, actually there is something I want to take Avery to do, if that's okay with you guys," Jason said with a sly smile plastered on his face.

Both of our mothers nodding in agreeance, and my mom gave my arm a comforting squeeze before heading out of the station together.

I was curious as to where Jason was taking me, and he wasn't giving me any clues. I was forced to come up with a million different scenarios, but thankfully each of them seemed positive. Twenty minutes later, we reached our destination. The smell of the ocean water hit my nostrils before I landed eyes on Brandon's favorite place, the beach.

I felt my eyes water, when I realized why Jason had brought me here. The last time we were here, we were at Brandon's memorial. We were still trying to figure out who killed Brandon, and we had brought Macy here. Looking back, it made me feel as if I had tarnished his memorial with her presence. I knew my friend would never see it that way, but needless to say I still felt bad.
*That disgusting bitch.*

We got out of the car, and Jason's hand found mine as we started down the steps to the sand. As our feet touched the course, cold sand, we were greeted with a bright orange sundown. This was the perfect time to come. I knew it was one of Brandon's favorite times of the day to be here, to relax against the sand, listening to the crashing waves relax, and watch the sun leave the sky. He always said it made him feel ready for the next day- ready to welcome tomorrow with open arms and an open heart.

"I wanted to bring you here, because while you haven't said anything, I know how you are feeling. You miss him, and I know we haven't had much time to unwind and say a final goodbye to our friend."

"That's just it, Jason. I don't want to say a final goodbye. I don't think that I will ever be ready to say goodbye to Brandon forever. It just doesn't feel right."

"I know what you mean. He should be surfing the last wave right now, and then complaining that it wasn't high or crazy enough for him," Jason said with a laugh.

"I want Brandon to know, that I will never forget him. I will remember him, his kind soul, and hid loud voice forever."

"Forever," Jason agreed and squeezed my hand.
*I miss you. So damn much.*

We laid down in the sand, and together watched the sun set, and felt a calming sensation wash over us. Tomorrow would be a new day, and we would welcome it with open arms. Just as Brandon would have wanted.

We remained there for what felt like hours, long after the sun had set. We finally pulled or aching bodies off the sand and brushed the remaining crystals off.

"Ready to go?" Jason asked with an outstretched hand.

"As I'll ever be," and my hand found his.

*This was what I always wanted. Jason and me.*

We bounded up the stairs, and into Jason's car. We decided to stop off at our favorite diner when we got back to town. This was becoming a tradition, and that was something I could get used to. Any time I spent with Jason, was something that I welcomed. I wanted to talk to Erica and Joey to fill them in on everything that happened this afternoon, especially because it was likely to be plastered all over the news tomorrow morning.

I sent a quick text: Hey guys, Jason and I are at Hal's. Meet us here?

They agreed and arrived no less than twenty minutes later. We rose to greet them, and they nearly tackled the both of us with hugs, then peeled themselves off, and swapped.

"Okay guys, don't forget I have some stitches that have already been irritated today."

They all laughed, and Joey pulled back slowly, holding me at arm's length and examining me for any more injuries.

"Hey! I am fine, okay? Maybe a little scratched up, but you should see the other girl," I said with a wink.

"I speak for both of us, when I say that I am so glad you're okay, and that they finally caught her. My mom said something about a gun?"

I launched into the long story that stemmed from Macy showing up at my home, escorting me out using a gun, taping me up, and holding me hostage at an abandoned building. I casually slipped in the part about me shooting her. As I went on, their mouths dropped more and more. I knew where they were coming from. If I hadn't lived it, then I don't know if I would exactly be believing it either.

Erica looked sad by the time my story finished. She grabbed my hand and looked at me somberly.

"I wanted to say how sorry I was again. You should have never been in prison to begin with, and Joey and I still feel responsible for that."

"Well, don't. Macy planted the shirt before you ever mentioned anything to Detective Greene. It was her plan even since she killed Brandon, to throw the blame on me. I have to hand it to her; she was very convincing."

"Yeah, I guess my mom talked to the policemen before we came out, and Macy's trial starts tomorrow," Jason added.

"Tomorrow? That's really soon."

"I guess so, but they have all the evidence they need. The fact that she stabbed you, and then ran away not only adds charges but, it means that they were ready to convict her. They just needed her."

We all sat there, thinking about the week's events. At least, that's what I was doing. I found myself being surprised when I said, "I want to visit her, when she's in prison."

My friends erupted into a fit of "Why's" and "Are you crazy's". I knew how they would react, and I wasn't going to see her because I felt any sort of pity for her. No, I wanted to tell her that I was glad she would spend the rest of her life behind bars, and that it would be the final time she ever saw me.

My friends grew silent, and I could tell they were pondering over whether or not to join me, stop me, or sit this one out altogether.

Jason was the first to add himself to the visiting list, and Erica and Joey shortly followed. That settled it. We would go tomorrow, after her first court date. I doubt it would take longer than one day to convict her. She was as guilty as they came.

We all ordered our food, and Jason and I practically devoured our entire plates. Joey and Erica opted for dessert, because they weren't in a crazy hostage situation earlier and had already eaten. When we finished, we paid for our bill, and left with the promise of seeing each other the following day.

The drive to my house was quieter than usual. Jason seemed to be lost in his own thoughts, a feeling I knew too well.

*Please tell me what you're thinking.*

It seemed as if he would read my mind, because he spoke. "Are you sure about this tomorrow? You have more reasons than any of us to hate her. I would be okay if you didn't want to go."

"Jason, it's my plan. I want to go. Think of this as "my final goodbye" to Macy. She is someone I could happily never see again. I want her to know that. Look, I know you are trying to protect me, but if the past few weeks have proven anything, it's that I am stronger than I look."

"Yes, you are," Jason said with a smile, as he pulled into my driveway.

He kissed my hand and got out and opened my door for me. "I will see you tomorrow, beautiful."

"See you, Jason," I said with a warm smile and started off to my front door. My mom greeted me right when I came in, and I saw that she wasn't alone.

The prosecutor was sitting right at the counter, sipping on a mug of tea.

"Hello, Avery. Your mom has been kind enough to allow me to wait for you until you returned. I don't want to impose on your evening but wanted to give you an update on everything that was happening with Macy."

I took a seat.

"What is it?"

"She has entered a guilty plea, and there is no need for a trial. Tomorrow, we will meet at the court for her sentencing. I am pushing for life with no parole. I just thought that was something you might want to know."

"That's great news. My friends and I were thinking of visiting her, one last time tomorrow."

"Well, I can understand why. I would advise you all to visit early in the morning, around nine a.m. Her court date isn't until 11 and sentencing can take a while longer."

I offered a "Thanks" and headed up to the bathroom to take a much-needed shower. I reminded myself to be careful with my stitches and getting them wet. It made showering much harder, but at this point, I didn't care.

I was cautious in the shower but relished in the feeling of the hot water on my back. I was adamant about a hot shower taking away all of my troubles, at least for the moment.

I stepped out and dried myself. I walked into my room and jumped nearly a foot back.

"Mom! You scared the crap out of me. Don't you know not to sneak up one someone who was recently stabbed and kidnapped?"

"That's what I wanted to talk to you about. Are you sure you want to do this tomorrow?"

"Mom, I need to do this. It is the only way I can properly begin to move on with my life."

"Okay, my love. I just want you to be careful."

I reminded my mother of the heavy amount of guards standing around us, and that I would be accompanied by my friends.

She finally ceded, kissed my head, and went to bed. For the first time in a while, my mind wasn't spinning around all the craziness, as it was finally calm. I could finally relax, in my bed, without the constant threat called Macy.

I fell asleep that night and dreamed of wonderful things. I was happy, even in my unconscious mind.

When I awoke in the morning, my body felt tired, but my mind felt more refreshed and awake then ever. I got dressed, and texted Joey and Erica to meet us at the prison in thirty minutes. I texted Jason and let him know I was ready.

He sent out a quick reply letting me know he was on his way. I also got confirmation from Joey and Erica that they would be leaving in ten minutes.

Jason honked the horn ten minutes later, and I ran out to the car. He was all smiles and waiting with a large coffee for me. *Dear lord, this man knew the way to my heart... and my stomach.*

I climbed into his car, and we started on our way to the prison. Surprisingly, I wasn't a jumbled mess of nerves. I was confident, and ready to move past all of this once and for all. After today, Macy would be a thing of the past. I would no longer be concerned with her, or her wellbeing. She was dead to me.

The car ride was a comfortable silence, which I liked. I needed to be alone with my thoughts for just a while longer.

I must have lost track of the time, because before I knew it- we had arrived. I saw Joey's car and urged Jason to park beside them. Once parked, all four of us scrambled out.

"I'm ready if you all are," I said with a confident smile.

Jason's hand found mine, and Joey's found Erica's. We were ready.

Once inside, we let the desk know that there were four visitors for Macy. They gave us name tags, and buzzed us in. We all took seats at this round table and waited for her to arrive. In no time at all, we spotted her. She was dressed in an orange jumpsuit, complete with a sinister look on her face. Glad to see the big house hadn't changed her too much.

"Well, well, well. Did you guys miss me already?"

"Just the opposite, actually. Sit," I motioned towards the empty side of the table.

She did as I asked and just stared at me blankly. She wasn't acknowledging anyone else, just had her eyes deadlocked on me. The days of her intimidating me were long gone, and I think she was beginning to realize that. Joey spoke.

"We all came here to tell you that we were done with you. We don't care what happens to you anymore, you're on your own."

"I have been on my own for quite a while now, I'm sure I can handle in," she said with a laugh.

"What you did to Avery is unforgivable. Killing Brandon was the worst thing you could have possibly done. You're a monster that we no longer want to associate with."

She went silent and looking at all of us.

"Brandon deserved it. They *all* deserved it."

We must have looked confused, because she continued.

"Oh, you thought Brandon was the only person I have ever killed?"

36518865R00090

Made in the USA
San Bernardino, CA
22 May 2019